Ms. Darcy had a wide, sincere smile.

"Weston High has just had a great honor bestowed upon it. Ours is the only school in Connecticut that has been invited to participate in a brand-new foreign exchange program. The students who participate will live with a French family in Paris so they can learn about life in another country."

Ms. Darcy's tone had grown serious. "It's not a simple decision to make. Yes, it sounds exciting—and even a little bit glamorous. But there are other factors to consider." The teacher looked around the room. "You need to think about what it would be like being on your own. How you would adjust to living far away from everything that's familiar to you. Whether or not you could feel comfortable in a country in which an entirely different language is spoken. All in all, it's a lot to take on."

Jennifer, Kristy, and Nina simply looked at each other. Not one of them said a word. But from the expressions on their faces it was clear that two of them were excited over the prospect of spending the summer in Paris, while the third was just plain bored.

A SUMMER IN PARIS

Cynthia Blair

FAWCETT JUNIPER • NEW YORK

RLI: $\dfrac{\text{VL 5 \& up}}{\text{IL 5 \& up}}$

A Fawcett Juniper Book
Published by Ballantine Books
Copyright © 1992 by Cynthia Blair

All rights reserved under International and Pan-American Copyright Conventions. Published in the United States by Ballantine Books, a division of Random House, Inc., New York, and simultaneously in Canada by Random House of Canada Limited, Toronto.

Library of Congress Catalog Card Number: 92-90152

ISBN 0-449-70393-2

Manufactured in the United States of America

First Edition: August 1992

To Emily Book

1

"BETTER WATCH OUT!" KRISTY CONNOR cried dramatically. "I just saw Ms. Darcy in the hall, and I could see from twenty feet away that she has that special gleam in her eye. You know, the one she always gets whenever she's about to spring a pop quiz on her favorite advanced French class."

"Oh, no! I sure hope not." With a loud groan, Jennifer Johnson glanced up, watching her friend as she plopped down at the desk right next to hers. "Cheerleading practice ran really late yesterday—until after five. The big game against Clinton High is next week, and we still have a zillion new cheers to learn. I got home so late that I didn't have a single *minute* to study those new irregular verbs Ms. Darcy just assigned."

"Are you sure it was only the big basketball game that was keeping you so busy?" Kristy teased, giving her wild red mane a toss in a useless attempt at keeping her hair out of her eyes. "Or was it the *captain* of the basketball team that kept you away from all those wonderful verbs?"

Jennifer giggled. She was a perky blue-eyed blonde, her pretty features complemented by the light makeup she always wore. That plus her interest in the trendiest clothes made her look as if

1

she had just stepped off the cover of *Sassy* magazine.

"Well . . . Danny and I *did* go out for a Coke afterward. The whole crowd was over at Burger 'n' Shake, talking about the big game. It was like the entire senior class had suddenly gotten a bad case of spring fever, and believe me, studying was the last thing on anybody's mind. I got home so late that my mother was ready to ground me." Jennifer rolled her eyes. "Fortunately, this was one time I managed to talk her out of it."

"I didn't study, either," Kristy said. "Nobody was home, and I just parked myself in front of the TV." She sighed. "Well, if we are having a surprise quiz, at least one of us is guaranteed to get an *A*." She gestured toward the pretty dark-haired girl sitting in front of her. "Right, Nina?"

Nina Shaw looked over her shoulder and smiled. As she turned, her shining dark brown hair, hanging down almost to her waist, caught the light, creating a shimmering effect.

"You know I don't mind studying French," she said, her large brown eyes shining with sincerity.

"Now *that's* an understatement if I've ever heard one," Kristy returned. "Nina, you love everything French. French cooking, French novels, French songs, French movies . . ."

"And don't forget those handsome French boys," Jennifer added with a grin. "I bet Nina would just love to meet some."

Before the dark-haired girl had a chance to reply, however, Ms. Darcy's voice interrupted the girls' friendly banter.

"If the three class chatterboxes can manage to stay quiet for a moment," their teacher said, striding toward the front of the classroom, "I'd like to make an announcement."

Jennifer, Kristy, and Nina reluctantly lapsed into silence. As they looked up, however, they were surprised to find that Ms. Darcy was smiling.

"No, this time it's not a quiz," she went on with a gentle laugh.

Ms. Darcy had a wide, sincere smile, which was just one of the many reasons she was one of the most popular teachers at Weston High School. She came around to the front of her desk, leaning against its edge as she continued addressing the class.

"What I have to say to all of you today is a lot more exciting than that. In fact, I've actually got some good news. Some *very* good news."

Jennifer and Kristy exchanged puzzled glances. Nina, meanwhile, leaned forward in her seat.

"Weston High has just had a great honor bestowed upon it. Ours is the only school in Connecticut that has been invited to participate in a brand-new foreign exchange program. It's being run by an organization called the Project for International Exchange."

David, one of the few juniors in the class, raised his hand. Without waiting for Ms. Darcy to call on him, he called out, "You mean kids from other countries are going to be coming to live in our town? They're coming here, to Weston?"

"Not exactly." Ms. Darcy hesitated, meanwhile glancing at all fourteen of her students. Everyone could sense the excitement in the room. "Actually, you, the students of Weston High's advanced French class, have been invited to spend this summer in Paris."

"Paris!" Nina exclaimed. "Paris, *France*?"

Ms. Darcy laughed. "That's the one I'm talking about. As part of an effort to bridge some of the gaps that exist between our culture here in the United States and the cultures of other countries, a handful of high schools have been chosen to send students who are interested in living abroad to foreign countries for the months of July and August. The students who participate will live with a French family in Paris so they can learn about life in another country."

She picked up a flyer from her desk, a sleek, colorful folder that looked like a travel brochure, and glanced at it. "The students who participate in the program will spend their mornings attending special classes at the Sorbonne, the finest university in Paris. Studying the language, the history, and the culture of France will help them get the most out of the experience."

"What about the afternoons?" David asked.

"Those are left free for sight-seeing, reading, studying—or whatever. The main purpose of the program is to allow young people to experience life in another country. How you spend your time is really up to you."

"Wow!" cried Sharon, who was sitting next to the bulletin board. On it were large colorful posters picturing some of the great castles of France. "Imagine spending the whole summer in France. Visiting these beautiful *chateaux*, the ones I've been drooling over since September. Seeing all that gorgeous countryside that the great artists painted, men like Claude Monet and women like Berthe Morisot. Touring the famous cathedrals and going

to the museums and eating French pastry all day
. . . Gosh, I can hardly wait! Where do I sign up?"

Ms. Darcy laughed. "I appreciate your enthusiasm, Sharon, and I hope that many of you will
decide to go. I certainly hope that all of you will
at least give it serious thought. It is, after all, the
chance of a lifetime. But there are some steps that
those students who are interested have to take."

"I get it," David broke in. "You mean like asking our parents' permission before we start pack-
ing our suitcases, right?"

"Something like that. That comes first. Then,
there are all kinds of forms to be filled out. There
are passport applications, questionnaires that will
help match you up with the host family that is best
for you. . . . I'm afraid that there's quite a bit of
paperwork involved.

"But the very first step is for each and every one
of you to think very carefully about whether or
not spending the summer living in Paris is right
for you."

Ms. Darcy's tone had grown serious. "It's not a
simple decision to make. Yes, it sounds exciting—
and even a little bit glamorous. It would provide
an unparalleled opportunity to learn—and not only
about the French language and culture, either.

"But there are other factors to consider." The
teacher looked around the room. "You need to
think about what it would be like being on your
own. How you would adjust to living far away
from everything that's familiar to you. Whether or
not you could feel comfortable in a country in
which an entirely different language is spoken.

"And then there's the problem of fitting in with
a brand-new family, one that's bound to bear little

resemblance to anything you're used to. All in all,
it's a lot to take on. And it's important to weigh
both the positives and the negatives."

Ms. Darcy paused to take a deep breath. "Now.
After all that, are there any questions?"

As Sharon and David and some of the others
bombarded their teacher with a dozen different
questions, Jennifer, Kristy, and Nina simply looked
at each other. Not one of them said a word. But
from the expressions on their faces it was clear
that two of them were excited over the prospect
of spending the summer in Paris, while the third
was just plain bored.

"I can hardly believe this is really happening,"
Nina said with a sigh as she and her two best
friends made their way across the expansive front
lawn of Weston High. Dreamily she kicked at the
dandelions just beginning to push their way up
through the stubby grass, barely noticing these
cheerful reminders that spring was on its way.
"I've been dying to see Paris for so long."

"At least as long as I've known you," Jennifer
said, flicking back her shoulder-length blond hair,
today held back on one side with a purple barrette
that exactly matched her sweater. "I remember
the very first day of junior high school, six long
years ago. You and I were in Mr. Thompson's beginning French class, and we ended up sitting next
to each other. You were positively thrilled to be
taking French.

"I was scared stiff. I never thought I'd be able
to learn another language. It just sounded too
hard." She wrinkled her nose. "The whole thing
was my parents' idea. They thought learning

French would make me more worldly or something."

"I remember that day, too," Kristy interrupted.
"Mr. Thompson went around the classroom, asking each one of us why we had signed up for French. I said something about how I'd heard it was easier to learn than German, and everybody laughed. But Nina, you went on and on about how much you wanted to learn about French poetry and art and all that stuff."

"Yeah, and that was all it took." Jennifer laughed. "After that, Mr. Thompson *loved* you. You were his favorite student in the class!"

"Well, who could blame him?" Kristy said. "I don't think Nina ever got a grade lower than a ninety-eight the whole three years she was in his class. Did you?"

Nina just smiled. "I've always had my reasons," she said. Then her smile faded, and she became quiet, making it clear that the subject was closed.

Jennifer and Kristy eyed each other knowingly. They were not at all surprised by their friend's mysterious behavior. Even though they had all been close ever since seventh grade, there had always been something about Nina Shaw that never let them forget she preferred to keep herself just a little bit separate from everyone else.

She was certainly well liked—one of the most popular girls at Weston High, in fact. And why wouldn't she be? The fact that she always had a kind word for everyone, despite her slight aloofness, made all the other girls want to be her friend. The boys, too—especially since she was also extremely pretty. With her long, shining dark hair, her large brown eyes, and her attractive, somewhat angular features, she caught the attention of some of the best-looking, most sought-after boys in school.

Even so, Nina chose not to spend too much time caught up in the social whirl. She had her friends, of course, especially Jennifer and Kristy. She dated often, although she had never paired off with one particular boy, the way Jennifer had with Danny. Nina valued her time alone, and she always made sure she kept part of her weekends for reading, taking long walks by herself, daydreaming—and writing.

"Well, one thing's for certain," Nina finally said. "I'm going to talk to my parents about this exchange program the very first chance I get. Hmmm, I wonder if I should whip up a chocolate *mousse* for dessert to help get them in the mood?"

Kristy and Jennifer laughed.

"I can't imagine your parents saying no to something like this," said Kristy. "I'm sure they'll know how important it is to you. Besides, didn't your mother used to live in France or something?"

"My grandmother," Nina replied. "She spent a year in Paris, studying art."

"Your grandmother?" Jennifer repeated. "Wow, that must have been ages ago."

Nina nodded. "It was. In the late 1930s, just before World War II."

"Well, this is where I turn off," Kristy said suddenly as the threesome reached the street corner whose location always demanded that they decide exactly who would be going home with whom. "Want to come over for a while?"

Jennifer was quick to agree. "Sure, I'd love to. Hey, I can show you the new cheers we've been practicing for the game next week. They're really awesome."

"Not me, thanks," Nina said, clutching her schoolbooks tightly against her chest. "I want to get home."

"Going to start making that chocolate *mousse*, huh?" Kristy teased.

Nina smiled. "Something like that. I'll see you both tomorrow."

"Right. 'Bye, Nina!"

"Good-bye. And good luck with your parents, Nina."

As Jennifer and Kristy turned down Emerson Street, they were both silent for a while. Finally, when Jennifer spoke, her voice sounded odd.

"What about you, Kristy? Are you interested in going on this exchange program thing?"

Kristy raised her eyebrows. "Well, sure, Jen. Aren't you?"

The blond girl shrugged. "I don't know. I mean, it sounds glamorous and all that. But this *is* my last summer here in Weston before I go away to college. Oh, sure, I'll be back to visit and all, but it'll never be quite the same. I've just been assuming I'd spend the summer here, hanging out with all my friends, maybe getting a summer job at one of the stores in town or over at the mall. . . ."

"And maybe seeing Danny once or twice?" Kristy teased.

"Well, sure." Jennifer cast her friend a clouded look. "Is it so strange that I want to spend the summer that way?"

"No, not at all. I understand how you feel. This trip to France sounds like fun to me—a little scary

maybe, like Ms. Darcy was saying, but still fun—
but I can see that it's not for everybody."

Jennifer sighed. "I just hope that Nina under-
stands, too."

"Nina? Why shouldn't she?" Kristy was truly
surprised by her friend's comment.

"Oh, you know how Nina is. She's so . . . so
romantic about things. She expects life to be the
way it is in books. Traveling all over the world,
meeting exciting people, eating out in fabulous
restaurants—"

"It sounds terrific to me!"

"I know, but it's not what *I* want. I'd be happy
just staying in Weston. To tell you the truth, I'm
even a little bit nervous about going away to college in Hartford in the fall." Jennifer shrugged her
shoulders. "I guess I'm just one of those people
who's not very adventurous. The idea of having to
face a lot of changes scares me." Nervously she
added, "So what do you think? Do you suppose
Nina will think I'm crazy for turning down a
chance to live in Paris for two months?"

Kristy slung a friendly arm around her friend's
shoulders. "Jennifer Johnson, I think you should
stop worrying about what Nina thinks—or anybody else, for that matter. We all have to do what's
right for us."

Instead of feeling relieved that Kristy understood her lack of interest in spending the summer
abroad, however, Jennifer was still bothered by a
tense, gnawing feeling in the pit of her stomach.
After all, she may have convinced one of her best
friends that she was only doing what she felt was
best for herself. But there were still two other people whom she would have to convince.

And convincing her mother and father of *anything* had never been very easy.

"Nobody's here," Kristy announced cheerfully after unlocking the front door of the Connors' spacious home and walking inside. She was not at all surprised, or the least bit disappointed. In fact, she was glad. She loved having the entire house to herself. She enjoyed the silence, the feeling of being on her own. Especially since lately it seemed that the rest of her family had no purpose in life other than to drive her crazy.

"Where is everybody?" Jennifer asked, following her into the kitchen.

"My dad's on one of his business trips. Want something to eat?"

"Sure. I figured your dad was working. But how about your mom and Kerry?"

Kristy just shrugged. "Oh, they're probably at some stupid audition." She opened the refrigerator and stuck her head inside. "All we have is ginger ale and root beer."

"Root beer. Wow, your little sister is at an audition? Where?"

"In New York, I guess. I don't bother to keep track anymore. Hey, look. Oreos!"

"Isn't it exciting, Kristy? Having a little sister who's a celebrity?"

As Kristy turned around to face her, a bottle of root beer in one hand and a package of Oreos in the other, there was an odd expression on her face. But before she had a chance to answer Jennifer's question, there was a commotion at the front door.

"Hi-i-i!" Kristy called.

"Hello!" Jennifer joined in.

But instead of having their greeting echoed, Jennifer heard Kristy's mother saying, "Now, Kerry, you'll *have* to add tap lessons. I know you already have ballet class, and of course there are your voice lessons, but it's absolutely essential that—"

As Ms. Connor and her eight-year-old daughter Kerry came into the kitchen, they both seemed startled to find Jennifer and Kristy there.

"Oh, hello, dear," Kristy's mother said. "I didn't realize you were home already." She cast a quick nod in Jennifer's direction. "Goodness, what time is it?"

"Three-thirty. The same time I always get home." Kristy sat down at the kitchen table, deliberately choosing a chair that forced her to turn her back on her mother and her sister.

Jennifer was puzzled. But she smiled and said, "Hi, Ms. Connor. Hi, Kerry. Gee, you sure are all dressed up. And is that makeup you've got on?"

"Of course." The little girl was wearing pigtails and more makeup than seventeen-year-old Jennifer had ever worn in her life. "I was at an audition."

"That's what Kristy thought. What were you auditioning for?"

"A Broadway play." The little girl tossed her head. "And I got the part."

"Wow!" Jennifer's blue eyes were wide. "You're going to be in a Broadway play?"

Kerry nodded. "I'm playing a six-year-old in a new musical. It's going to be the hit of the season."

"Golly, that's terrific!" Jennifer glanced over at Kristy and saw that she was keeping her eyes down and at the same time stuffing Oreos into her mouth as fast as she could.

"Well, you shouldn't be surprised, Jennifer, dear," Ms. Connor said coolly. "It's not as if Kerry hasn't been doing plays and even television since she was four. You have seen her cereal commercial, haven't you?"

"Sure. Everybody in Weston knows that Kerry is practically a star. But a Broadway play? Gee!"

"I thought it was *off*-Broadway," Kristy mumbled. "Or maybe even off-off-Broadway."

Her mother didn't seem to have heard her. "Kristy, did you read Kate's letter? I left it on the dining room table. She has some wonderful news."

"I can hardly wait to hear it," Kristy muttered. Jennifer was taken aback by her sullen tone, but once again, her mother acted as if she hadn't even heard her.

"Yes, your big sister has been nominated for May queen at her college. She sent a clipping from the school newspaper. Her picture was on the front page. It's such an honor. Any one of the sorority girls would have given her eyeteeth to be May queen. Of course, it's not as if her father and I haven't been expecting it all along."

"Mom, since I'm going to be a famous Broadway actress," Kerry interrupted, her voice an irritating whine, "does that mean I can get some new clothes? I think I deserve a whole new wardrobe."

"Of course," Ms. Connor replied without hesitating for a moment. She leaned down and planted a quick kiss on top of her youngest daughter's head. "Whatever you want, Kerry. Nothing is too good for my Broadway star."

"Something interesting happened at school today," Kristy said, finally turning around to face her mother. "The kids who are taking Ms. Darcy's advanced French class have been invited to spend the summer in Paris. The deal is that you live with a French family, studying the language at the Sorbonne and living in a different culture. It would be a great way for me to spend the summer before I go off to college in Boston in the fall."

"Why, Kristy, that's just wonderful!" Ms. Connor's face lit up, and there was real enthusiasm in her voice.

"It is?" Kristy looked at her, blinking. "You mean you're really excited about my having an opportunity like this?"

"It sounds perfect. It lasts all summer?"

"That's right. July and August."

"It's ideal, Kristy. I'd been worrying about how I'd manage this summer, what with having to take Kerry back and forth to New York for this play. Sending you abroad is the perfect solution."

Already Ms. Connor had turned away. "Now, come on upstairs, Kerry. It's important that you start learning how to remove your makeup properly. Here, let me give you a lesson."

When they were gone, Kristy looked at Jennifer and smiled sadly.

"See that?" she said, her green eyes shining with tears she wasn't about to let fall. "I just knew that when my mom found out how important this Paris thing was to me, she wouldn't hesitate to say yes."

It was past six by the time Jennifer slunk into her own house. The two cars in the driveway told her that her parents were already home. Her mother, Louise Johnson, was back from New York City, where she was a partner in a law firm. Her father, Dr. Paul Johnson, had apparently already finished seeing the day's patients at the office in town that he shared with two other psychologists.

She intended to delay talking to them, planning to slip upstairs to her bedroom so she could buy herself a little more time. But the moment she placed her foot on the first step, her mother popped into the front hall from the kitchen.

"Oh, hi, Jennifer. I thought I heard you come in."

"Hi, Mom." Longingly Jennifer glanced at the staircase. So much for her escape.

"Listen, Dad picked up a pizza on his way home. He and I are just setting up in the kitchen. Why don't you come and join us?"

Reluctantly she followed her mother into the kitchen, where her father was carefully putting forks and napkins next to the plates he had already set at each place at the table.

"Hi, sweetie," he greeted her as she came in. "How was school today?"

"Fine." Jennifer dropped into a kitchen chair.

"I'm just reheating this pizza," her mother said. "It'll be ready in about three minutes." Louise Johnson's eyes were twinkling. "But in the meantime, I have some incredible news that I'm just dying to tell you. Jen, you'll never guess who I ran into at the train station this evening."

"Who, Mom?"

"The principal of your school, that's who. And Mr. Kramer had something very exciting to tell me."

Jennifer could feel her heart sinking down

somewhere into her stomach. "Oh, really?" she asked. But she already knew what was coming.

"Paul, wait until you hear this," Louise Johnson said to her husband. "Oh, sweetie, I'm so glad that I'm the one to tell you about this terrific surprise." She took a deep breath. "Weston High has been asked to participate in an international exchange program. The seniors who are taking Ms. Darcy's advanced French class have been invited to spend the summer in Paris, studying at the Sorbonne and living with a French family. Isn't that fantastic?"

"I already knew all about it, Mom," Jennifer said. "My French teacher made an announcement in class today."

Her mother looked surprised. "You already knew? Goodness, then why didn't you say anything when you first came in? Surely you didn't think your father and I would say no to a wonderful opportunity like this, did you?" she added, beaming.

"No, I didn't think that." Jennifer picked up her paper napkin and nervously began folding it over and over again. "Mom, this might come as a great surprise to you, but I didn't plan on saying anything about the Paris thing because, well, I don't want to go."

"You don't want to go!" both her parents cried at the same time. They sounded like a chorus. Jennifer would have started laughing if she hadn't been bracing herself for what she knew was coming.

She took a deep breath. "Mom, Dad, I want to stay here in Weston this summer."

"Here . . . in Weston?" Dr. Johnson repeated, incredulous.

"Jennifer, what are you saying?" Her mother looked stunned. "Surely you can't mean it. Why, any girl in her right mind would jump at the chance—"

"I'm not 'any girl!' I'm me. And not only am I not jumping at the chance, I can't think of anything I'd rather do *less*."

"But why?" Dr. Johnson demanded, still puzzled. "I don't understand."

"Look, this is my last summer before college. All I want to do is stay home, get a summer job in town, see my friends, spend time with Danny. . . ."

"Oh, is *that* all." Ms. Johnson sounded relieved. "You're afraid you'll miss Danny. Or maybe that he'll find another girlfriend while you're gone. Well, honey, I can assure you that Danny is just a high school romance, a sweet case of puppy love that you'll soon begin to see as nothing more than—"

"It's not puppy love!" It was all Jennifer could do to keep from leaping out of her chair. "Danny and I really care about each other! It's not fair of you to say something like that. Besides, if I'm old enough to go to France by myself, then I'm certainly old enough to decide how I want to spend my summer!"

"You do have a point," her father said. Her mother, meanwhile, was nodding.

Jennifer was annoyed at how calm they were—and how irritating she was finding them at this moment. She would have found it more satisfying if they had started yelling at her. Instead, they were logical, thoughtful . . . and totally in control. That was the problem with having a father who was a psychologist and a mother who was a lawyer. Between the two of them, they were always at least two steps ahead of her.

"I'm sure I speak for your father when I say that we both understand how you're feeling right now," Louise Johnson said. "This is a difficult, confusing time for you. Of course you feel strong ties to your childhood. You're not sure if you're ready to grow up."

"Resistance to growing up and being on your own is very common," her father chimed in. "In many ways it's a terrifying prospect."

"I can't stand it when you go all analytical and understanding on me," Jennifer mumbled.

"Your mother and I both know that this whole time is difficult for you, honey," her father said. "But it's about time you spread your wings a little. You're almost eighteen, and it's time to leave the nest, to venture out into the world a bit—"

"I'm not a blue jay, for goodness sake!" Jennifer cried. "And I don't see what's wrong with being happy exactly where I am."

"What's wrong with it," her mother said calmly, "is that people don't grow unless they take a few risks. You can't spend your whole life hiding in a little town like Weston, Connecticut."

"I *am* going to Hartford in the fall," Jennifer reminded them meekly, but her words went unnoticed.

"Goodness, Jennifer," her mother was saying, "the chance to live abroad, to expand your horizons, to feel comfortable somewhere other than the place in which you grew up. . . ."

"Dad?" Jennifer looked at him with desperation in her blue eyes.

"I'm with your mother on this, sweetie. You've never been one to look very far outside yourself and your own experience. For a while now I've been feeling you need to go a bit beyond your small circle of friends, your cheerleading squad, the security of what you've always known. There's a big world out there, and you owe it to yourself to find out what it's like. And this summer program sounds like just the thing to get you started."

Jennifer looked from her father to her mother, then back to her father. She knew them well enough by now to be able to translate the expressions on their faces. And one thing was very clear: like it or not, she would be wise to start brushing up on her French vocabulary.

"Je vais à Paris," Nina Shaw happily sang as she cleared the table of the coffee cups and dessert dishes, noting with satisfaction that her chocolate *mousse* had been completely devoured. "I'm going to Paris. I'm really going. *Je vais à Paris.*"

She had barely been able to eat dinner as she waited until dessert to spring her big news on her parents. Ms. Darcy's announcement was all she could think about as her younger brother filled the family in on every last detail of the horror movie he and his friends had watched on TV after school that afternoon. As she tried to force herself to eat, she actually pinched herself a few times, just to be certain she wasn't dreaming.

But she wasn't dreaming. It was real. Just as real as the fact that her parents had finally agreed to let her go.

They hadn't been very enthusiastic at first.

"Paris?" her father had repeated, blinking hard. "Paris, France?"

"Yes, Dad. Paris, France," Nina had replied, laughing. She could remember having said those exact same words herself, not that long before.

As usual, her mother and father were full of doubts. Nina wasn't surprised. By this point in her life, she was fully prepared for her parents' timidness about stepping off the straight and narrow path.

Both of them, she knew, had always been perfectly happy with doing nothing more than working and taking care of their house. They found great comfort in always doing the same things, following the same routine, never taking any risks. Even on their infrequent vacations they never did anything more adventurous than visit some tourist spot like Williamsburg, Virginia, or Disney World. Even then, they invariably insisted upon staying at a Holiday Inn and eating all their meals in familiar chain restaurants and fast food places. And from what she could tell, her younger brother was turning out exactly the same way.

She, meanwhile, had always been the dreamer of the family. She was the one who longed to travel, to try new things . . . to experience life as fully as she possibly could. And so she had all her arguments ready for what was bound to come after she told them her news.

"Paris," her father continued muttering, shaking his head in disbelief.

Her mother was at least willing to try to understand. "Well," she said slowly, "it is true that going to France has been Nina's dream for as long as any of us can remember."

"Yes, and now it's finally going to happen." Nina was quick to add, "That is, if you'll let it happen."

Mr. Shaw frowned as he turned to face his wife. "But Emily, Paris, France? It's so far away."

"It's not as if I won't be able to manage in another country," Nina was quick to point out. "My French is good enough for me to get by, and I'm sure I'll pick up even more in a very short time."

"But . . ."

"And if I'm going to get serious about becoming a writer—which you both know is what I really want to do—I think it's very important for me to spend some time in Europe. And Paris is such a cultural center that it's the ideal place."

"Nina, I don't think you . . ."

"And I know I had planned to get a summer job to help pay my college expenses in the fall. But I do have a scholarship, and I'll be getting a part-time job once school gets started. Besides, I'm going to a college that's so close to Weston that I'll be living at home for at least the first year. We all agreed that that made the most sense, since going to school there was guaranteed to keep my expenses low."

Nina paused to take a deep breath. "Given all that, I just know I'll manage somehow."

"And the cost of the trip?" her mother asked. "You know that we're not wealthy people, Nina."

"The cost of the trip," Nina said matter-of-factly, glad she had already thought all this out, "will be covered by the inheritance Grandma left me."

Her parents' mouths dropped open. Nina knew then that she had made them see that despite their own reservations, in the end there was really nothing they could do to stand in her way.

"My birthday is in just two more weeks," Nina went on, "and you've been telling me for years that Grandma left me some money to be given to me when I turned eighteen. You always said she had made a point of saying it was to be used in any way I chose. And since Grandma herself spent a year in Paris, studying painting, I'm sure she'd be thrilled to have me use the money she left me for the same purpose."

In the end, her parents had agreed. They were still worried, but they recognized their daughter's determination. Nina, meanwhile, was already making plans. In her head she was drawing up lists of what she would pack, what she would need to do before she left, which addresses she should bring for the long letters she intended to send back.

But there was something else she simply had to do. Immediately after finishing up in the kitchen, she went upstairs to the second floor of the Shaws' house, then continued up to the third floor.

The attic was dusty, filled with old junk that nobody ever bothered with anymore. Nina couldn't remember the last time either of her parents had been up there.

To Nina, however, it was a special place. Stacked up behind the old clothes and the ice skates that no longer fit anyone and the cartons of her old art projects from elementary school, there was a heavy wooden trunk. It had belonged to her grandmother, and it was one more thing that Anna Wentworth had left to her favorite grandchild.

Nina went over to it and opened it up. Lovingly she lifted out the old clothes, the fanciful hats, the albums filled with black-and-white photographs. And then, after pausing to make sure no one was coming up, she reached down to the bottom of the trunk. With great care she pulled out the real treasure her grandmother had left her, the secret that only her beloved granddaughter had shared—and even then, not until Nina's grandmother had died.

As she took out the small bundle and held it in her hands, Nina's eyes filled with tears.

"This is for you," she said aloud, her voice catching even though she was only speaking in a whisper. "Don't worry, Grandma. Wherever you are, I want you to know that I haven't forgotten. I'm going to Paris. Finally, hopefully, I'll be able to put things right."

2

"I CAN'T BELIEVE MY PARENTS ARE REALLY making me go through with this." wailed Jennifer Johnson. "Oh, Danny, how am I ever going to live without you for two whole months?"

"Well, Jen, I'm afraid we're both going to have to find a way to deal with being apart—and pretty darned fast, too."

Danny glanced around at the crowds surrounding him at New York City's busy John F. Kennedy Airport. Throngs of people were rushing by, lugging heavy suitcases, periodically checking the tickets and passports that were tucked into their pockets. Most of them looked happy, filled with anticipation about the trips they were about to take. He and Jennifer were definitely the exception.

"I'm going to write to you every single day," Jennifer insisted. She swatted at the tears streaming down her cheeks, no longer concerned about whether or not her mascara was running. "I'll write *twice* a day."

"And I'll write back," Danny promised. "Look, it's only eight weeks. The time is going to whiz right by. You'll see. Now come on, Jen. It's not the end of the world. Be brave."

Jennifer took a deep breath and nodded. "Okay, I'll be brave." And then she burst into tears once

24

again, burying her head in Danny's shoulder and holding on so tightly it looked as if she had no intention of ever letting go.

"I feel like I'm watching my favorite soap opera," Kristy commented, glancing over in their direction from where she and Nina were sitting inside the waiting area of Gate 15. "I haven't seen this much drama since Brent Hayworth on 'The World is Wide' left Courtney Calloway to join the Peace Corps."

Nina laughed. "Come on, Kristy. Have a heart. Jennifer is really torn up about this. And leaving Danny behind is only part of it. You know as well as I do that she simply doesn't want to go."

"Well, as far as I'm concerned, this is the most exciting thing that's ever happened to me. To any of us, in fact. I've been waiting for this day for weeks. Ever since I first found out about this summer program, it's just about the only thing I've been able to think about."

"I know exactly what you mean," Nina said. "I haven't been able to think about anything else, either."

The girls weren't exaggerating. It had been a busy spring, what with the Senior Prom, final exams, and, finally, graduation. But through it all, the main concern of more than half the students in Ms. Darcy's advanced French class had been getting ready for their summer in Paris. They were all excited as they shopped for clothes, got their paperwork in order, and brushed up on their French.

Instead of merely memorizing vocabulary words and conjugating verbs, Nina and Kristy had gotten together two or three times a week to work on their French together. They learned phrases that would be helpful on their trip. They practiced talking to each other, using only French as they did the simplest things: strolling at the mall, going to McDonald's, discussing what they planned to wear to a particular school event.

Nina cast one more glance at Jennifer and Danny, who were still clinging to each other. With a sigh, she said, "I just hope that once we get there, Jennifer can stop being mad at her parents long enough to have some fun."

"Attention!" a voice suddenly crackled over the loudspeaker. "Air France Flight Number Seventy, New York City to Paris, is now boarding at Gate fifteen. Will passengers with boarding tickets for rows thirty-five through fifty please—"

Kristy nearly jumped out of her seat. "Well, Nina, this is it!" she cried excitedly, reaching for her carry-on bag.

"Yes," Nina said, her dark eyes glowing, "this really is it."

She could hardly believe it was actually happening. But as she gathered up her things to board the plane, there was no mistaking the fact that what had been just a dream for so long was now about to become a reality.

"*Attention, Mesdames et Messieurs.* Ladies and gentlemen, may I please have your attention. Now that Air France Flight Number Seventy has landed at Charles de Gaulle Airport, we ask that you please remain seated with your seat belts fastened until—"

"We're here." Nina's eyes were glowing as she pressed her face against the cool glass of the airplane window. Instead of feeling tired after her six-hour flight from New York, she was exhilarated, buoyed up by a sudden burst of energy. "We're in Paris!"

"*This* is Paris?" Jennifer, sitting right beside her, groaned. "Great. It's raining."

"Oh, it's just a little summer shower," insisted Kristy, sitting across from them on the aisle. "Besides, I think it's kind of romantic."

She leaned across Jennifer so she could get a better look at the activity on the airport runway as the plane neared the passenger terminal. "Oooh, look at all those French people," she squealed. "Gosh, I can hardly wait to talk to them. Do you think they'll really understand me when I say, *'Bonjour, Monsieur. Comment allez-vous?'* "

"Not with that accent," Jennifer grumbled.

"Come on, Jen," Nina said gently. "Don't tell me you're not even a little bit excited about being in Paris. Just think, this is the home of the Louvre Museum and Napoleon's tomb and the palace of Versailles. . . ."

Jennifer scowled. "All I can think about right now is Danny. I wonder what he's doing at this exact moment."

"If he has any sense at all," Kristy returned, "he's fast asleep. Back home, it's still the middle of the night. Don't forget, here it's six hours later than it is in Connecticut."

"And here," Nina said, turning her face back to the window, "the city of Paris is just beginning to wake up. But just think: today, we're all a part of it."

The girls spent the next two hours in a daze. Between jet lag and their disbelief that they were finally in Paris, Nina, Jennifer, Kristy, and the other five students from their class who were spending their summer abroad were like robots as they followed Ms. Darcy around the airport. They had their passports checked, retrieved their luggage from the revolving carousel, and waited in line to change American dollars into French francs.

"Look at the funny money," Kristy cooed. Her eyes were wide as she examined the handful of exotic-looking coins and colored bills the teller had just handed her. "It looks like a kid's toy."

"Wait until you start spending it." Jennifer made a face. "I bet you'll find it only goes about as far as a kid's toy, too."

Nina and Kristy just looked at each other and shrugged.

Riding from the airport into the city with their other classmates gave the girls the chance to catch their first real glimpse of the city that for the next two months would be their home. First they drove along highways, congested roads from which they could see little more besides billboards—all of them, much to the girls' delight, in French. Then, finally, the airport bus began making its way through the outermost streets of the city. Both Nina and Kristy were beside themselves with glee.

"Look at the shops," Kristy squealed, pressing her nose more tightly against the bus window. "Aren't they cute? *Boucherie*—that's the butcher shop."

"And look over there," Nina chimed in. "*Épicier*. That's the corner grocery."

"Oh, look!" cried Kristy. "A *pâtisserie*. Ummm, I can't wait to go into one of those. I love French pastry, and I can't wait to try the authentic version!"

"And there's another French eating place," Jennifer observed, showing more enthusiasm than she had since they had arrived. "I'm going to make a point of trying that one!"

Her two friends turned to look where she was pointing—and saw that they had just gone past Kentucky Fried Chicken.

Nina laughed. "See that, Jen? Maybe it won't be so bad here, after all. I mean, how can you get homesick when a little bit of home has followed you here?"

Ms. Darcy, their chaperone and tour guide, had announced back at the airport that the students would be dropped at a central point at the Sorbonne, the city's famed university on the trendy Left Bank. Their host families would also be there, waiting to pick up their houseguests for the summer. As the airport bus turned down the Left Bank's main thoroughfare, Boulevard St. Germaine, Kristy began to think less about the city— and more about her brand-new "family."

"Gosh, I hope I like the people I'm staying with," she remarked as the bus jerked to a halt in front of a large stone building, one of the many buildings making up the Sorbonne's far-flung campus. "I've been so wrapped up in the idea of coming to Paris that I haven't given much thought to my host family. I wonder what they'll be like."

"I just hope mine can cook American-style food," Jennifer commented. "Hot dogs, hamburgers . . . none of those weird sauces and funny-looking desserts for me."

She stood up quickly, banging her head on the

luggage rack up above. "Oh, darn," she cried, her voice filled with exasperation. "What I wouldn't give for a Twinkie right about now."

"Well, I hope my host family is very, very French," Nina said firmly. "I don't intend to speak a word of English while I'm here—except to you two, of course. And if my family has even a single Twinkie in their house . . ."

"Just save it for me, will you?" Jennifer pleaded, rubbing the top of her head.

The host families had already gathered inside the small auditorium as the students filed in, looking tired but hopeful as they dragged along their suitcases. Ms. Darcy, looking surprisingly fresh, immediately took charge.

"All right, everybody," she said, speaking in English. "I know you're all exhausted from the flight, and I'm sure you're eager to meet your host families and get settled. First I'll call off the name of each student, and then I'll call the name of the family with whom he or she will be staying. The student and the family can meet up front, right here." She repeated her instructions in French.

The girls held their breath as they waited for their names to be called. Kristy was first. Her family, she was glad to see, consisted of a youthful couple with two children, little girls aged about eight and ten. Madame and Monsieur LeBlanc spoke excellent English, and their daughters Nicole and Sophie, they announced, were looking forward to learning it over the summer.

Next, Nina was matched up with a middle-aged couple who had no children but had spent some time living in America. They were pleased that they would have the chance to brush up on their English over the summer—even though Nina insisted right up front that she would prefer speaking nothing but French in their home.

Finally, every name had been called except Jennifer's. She stood alone, looking forlorn, watching her friends and classmates happily going off with their new "families." A knot was forming in her stomach. A wave of homesickness—of fear—began to spread over her with alarming speed.

I don't want to be doing this, she thought, blinking hard, trying her hardest not to do anything as silly as start bawling like a baby. All I ever wanted to do was to stay at home where I'm safe and happy and—

"Jennifer Johnson!" Ms. Darcy called. She was smiling as Jennifer looked over at her, blinking in surprise at finally having heard her name called. "Jennifer, you're the last one on my list. You'll be staying with Henri and Rose Cartier."

Anxiously Jennifer looked around, trying to catch sight of her new family. She hoped they would have children, like Kristy's family, or that they would at least be cheerful and bubbly, like Nina's.

But her heart sank when she caught sight of the Cartiers. They were an older couple, probably in their late seventies, dressed in rather shabby clothes that looked as if they hadn't been in style for ages. Henri and Rose stood together holding on to each others' arms, their eyes darting about as they searched for their new "daughter."

"Madame, Monsieur," Ms. Darcy was saying, "I would like to introduce your houseguest for the summer, Jennifer Johnson."

Jennifer felt like bursting into tears. But instead,

she blinked hard, picked up her suitcases, and forced a weak smile. Already she was counting the number of days she would have to stay here in Paris before she would be allowed to go back home again. And from the way things were going, it looked like it was going to be an even longer summer than she had expected.

The Cartiers' house, just as Jennifer had feared, was very much like the couple themselves. They lived in one of the more run-down sections of Paris, in a modest apartment that didn't get very much sunlight. It consisted of four compact rooms: a living room, a kitchen, and two tiny bedrooms, one for her and one for the Cartiers.

"Uh, where is the bathroom?" Jennifer asked nervously, looking around for a doorway she had somehow missed. *"Où est la toilette?"*

"Right down the hall," Madame Cartier informed her in French, smiling. "Not far at all."

I simply have to get out of here, Jennifer decided then and there. I'm going to have to go home, that's all. There's absolutely no reason in the world to get upset about this. The very first chance I get, I'll call my parents, collect. I'll go out to a pay phone, where the Cartiers can't hear me— even though it appears that they don't speak a word of English. Once I explain the situation to Mom and Dad, I'm sure they'll let me come home.

For the moment, however, Jennifer was left to make the best of things.

"You must be tired," Henri Cartier said in a kind voice after proudly showing her around the apartment. "Would you like to rest?"

"Yes, thank you. That's an excellent idea."

Jennifer was only too happy to retreat to her small bedroom. It overlooked a courtyard. In it, someone had planted a small garden. It was flourishing, with colorful flowers blooming and hearty vegetables pushing their way out of the ground. Obviously it was the project of someone quite dedicated to making things grow.

But Jennifer wasn't thinking about gardens as she lay down on the creaky cot, certain that she would never be able to sleep. Not now, when the thing she had been so dreading was finally coming to pass—and it was turning out even worse than she had ever expected. She was miserable, hardly able to believe she had gotten herself into this unbearable situation. But she was exhausted from her trip, and before long she sank into a deep sleep.

When she opened her eyes once again, it took her a few seconds to remember where she was. And when she did, that same sick feeling returned. She sat up abruptly, noticing that the sun had shifted radically while she had been asleep. Jennifer knew then that she had been asleep for a long time.

She looked around the room, noting that for some reason things looked different. Someone had tried to make it look more homey.

A quick look around told her that, while she had been asleep, someone had come in and unpacked her suitcases. All her clothes were hanging in the closet or folded neatly inside the drawers of the empty dresser next to her bed. There was a pitcher of water and a glass on the dresser. Next to them was a jar filled with a bouquet of fragrant fresh flowers, probably from the small garden out back.

Blinking hard, partly in confusion, partly from

having just woken up, Jennifer wandered out of the bedroom and into the living room. She found Madame Cartier sitting in a sagging stuffed chair, reading.

"Ah, you are awake," she said, rising to her feet. "Did you have a good rest?"

"Yes, very good." Jennifer felt silly speaking in French, but she realized that she had no choice. "What time is it?"

"It is just past three."

"Three! I practically slept the whole day away!"

Madame Cartier chuckled. "It is very tiring, flying halfway across the world. Come into the kitchen. I have made you something to eat. You must be very hungry by now."

Jennifer was hungry, but she was a bit fearful about what strange foods might be set before her. She remembered the time her parents had taken her to a fancy French restaurant in New York. It was supposed to be in celebration of her birthday, but in truth she would have preferred going to a place where she could get a nice, plain steak.

As it turned out, she ate little more besides rolls. The dishes she and her parents ordered were so unappealing to her that she couldn't bring herself even to try them.

So she was not exactly looking forward to the lunch that Rose Cartier had prepared for her. And when the woman motioned for her to sit down at the kitchen table and then brought her a plate full of food, Jennifer's worst fears were realized.

"This is a very nice goat cheese," the woman explained, pointing to one of the oddly shaped, unappetizing items on the plate. "And this is *pâté*—

you know, goose liver paste. Very special, but then again, you are our very special guest."

Well, at least I can eat the crackers, Jennifer was thinking. But Rose Cartier sat down at the table right opposite her, beaming and watching her as she poured her some tea from a chipped ceramic teapot.

"Ah, let me show you," she finally said, misinterpreting Jennifer's reluctance to try the new foods as confusion. Patiently the older woman spread some of the cheese onto a cracker, then put some *pâté* on another. "Here, try this," she said, holding it out toward Jennifer.

Well, I guess it won't kill me. . . . Jennifer reached for the crackers, so hungry that she decided that some food—any food—was better than none. If I can only get this down without choking. . . . I just hope that tea isn't too hot to help me wash it down in a hurry.

Nervously she bit into the cracker with the goat cheese. She was bracing herself for the worst. But much to her amazement, she found it was actually tasty. It was delicious, in fact.

"Ummm," she said, gobbling down the rest of the cracker. "Madame Cartier, this is good!"

And the *pâté*, she discovered, after tasting it with the same caution, was also excellent.

"Ah, I am so glad you like it," Madame Cartier said sincerely. She was all smiles as she continued to watch Jennifer eat. "You know, my husband and I have so been looking forward to your visit. It is very important to us that you have a good summer here. I know that we are not young people, and that our home is very simple. . . ."

"Uh, it's fine. It's very nice, in fact. Really."

Jennifer was astonished to find herself trying to allay the woman's fears. Especially since, as far as she was concerned, she still planned to do everything she could to get herself out of this situation as fast as possible.

"Well, please let Henri and I know if there is anything we can do to make your stay here more enjoyable," Madame Cartier continued.

Jennifer just nodded. She was too busy devouring the rest of the goat cheese and *pâté* to answer.

"Jennifer? Is that really you?"

Louise Johnson was beside herself with glee over picking up the telephone and finding herself talking to her daughter, some three thousand miles away. Jennifer, meanwhile, was relieved by her mother's reaction. She had been away from home for only twenty-four hours, and she was afraid that her parents would be irritated by the fact that she was already calling home—collect, no less.

"Hold on a second, Jen. Your father is going to pick up the extension—Paul, is that you?"

"It's me, honey. I'm on. Jennifer, how are you?"

"I'll bet you're calling to tell us how fabulous Paris is," her mother quickly interrupted. "Oh, sweetie, didn't we tell you you'd love it? It's a beautiful, wonderful city, easily the most romantic place in the entire—"

"Mom, I really have to get out of here," Jennifer announced. While she had intended to sound matter-of-fact, perhaps even angry, her voice instead came out sounding terrified. She was on the verge of tears. And sounding desperate, she knew, was no way to win her parents over.

"Now, Jen," her mother was saying consolingly, "what could be so terrible?"

"It sounds like you're just a little bit homesick," Mr. Johnson added, chuckling.

"You don't understand!" Jennifer blurted out. "It's . . . it's horrible! The family they've got me staying with is just awful. They're these two old people, and they hardly speak a word of English. . . ."

"How wonderful!" Louise Johnson said. "By the time you come home in eight weeks, you'll be speaking like a native."

"What an opportunity," her husband chimed in.

"But Dad! The bathroom is down the *hall*! I mean, it's not even in the apartment!"

Paul Johnson was chuckling once again. "It sounds just like the place your mother and I stayed in during our first trip. Remember, Louise? Our feet would be killing us from a long day of sightseeing, and then we'd come back to our hotel and find that we had to—"

"Surely you don't expect me to live in a place with no bathroom!" Jennifer shrieked. She was aware that the people on the street corner on which she was standing as she made this long-distance plea for help were eyeing her oddly. But she didn't care. All she did care about, in fact, was getting her point across to her parents.

"Oh, honey, I know it's all new to you," Louise Johnson was saying. "It will take some getting used to."

"Of course it will." Dr. Johnson was, as usual, only too happy to agree with his wife. "But I guarantee that in a week—no, no, make that two or three days—you'll be tripping along the streets of Paris, considering it your second home."

"Oh, Daddy . . ."

"Now listen, young lady. This telephone call is going to cost a fortune. I want you to try to put all your fears aside and tackle this thing head on. Think of it as a challenge."

"An opportunity," came her mother's voice.

"A chance to experience something brand new. We know you can do it, Jen. We love you, and we have a lot of faith in you."

Before she knew it, her parents had said their cheerful good-byes and hung up. Jennifer was left standing on a street corner in Paris, holding on to a dead phone.

This, she thought, has got to be one of the low points of my life.

But instead of simply giving up, she started rummaging through her purse, looking for the list of telephone numbers Ms. Darcy had handed out that morning. Right now, what she needed was some moral support. And the best place to find that, she knew, was in familiar territory.

"I'm telling you, it's like something out of a horror movie," Jennifer complained loudly, tugging at a strand of her blond hair in irritation. "In the first place, the apartment is about as big as a closet. In the second place, it doesn't even have a bathroom. In the third place—"

"Oh, Jennifer, it sounds romantic to me," Nina insisted. She dropped down onto one of the benches in the long main gallery of the Musée d'Orsay, Paris's modern art museum and the place the three girls had agreed to meet on the morning of their second day in Paris. "Of course, Jacques and Isabelle Rousseau have been absolutely wonderful to me, and their town house on the Left Bank is like something out of a magazine. But they're so anxious to brush up on their English that I actually feel guilty speaking to them in French."

"I know what you mean," Kristy said, joining her on the bench. "The LeBlancs are so pleased to have someone around who can help their two daughters learn English. I feel like I owe it to them." She made a face. "The only problem is that I'm not going to learn much French."

"Come *on*!" Jennifer wailed. "You've got to be kidding! Do you have any idea what it's like having to speak French morning, noon, and night?"

Her two friends looked at her in surprise.

"But Jennifer!" Kristy said. "That's what we came here for."

"That's not what I came here for," Jennifer grumbled. "Look, it's certainly no secret that the only reason I'm here is that my parents forced me to come. And I can see that the only way I'm ever going to get through this endless summer is if you spend every free minute you have with me. I happen to need a couple of really good friends right now."

Nina and Kristy exchanged alarmed glances.

"But Jen," Kristy began.

Nina was quick to intercede. "Jennifer, I know you're feeling a little unsettled right now. And it's no surprise, since we've only just gotten here. Everything is strange, everything is new . . . and it seems like you're really disappointed in your host family."

Jennifer rolled her eyes upward. "Now *that's* a real understatement."

"But do me a favor. . . . No, wait. Do yourself a favor. Give it some time, Jen. Don't decide so quickly that you're miserable here or that you don't like the Cartiers. Try to be open-minded. Try to give it a chance."

"Sure, Nina, that's easy for you to say," Jennifer returned. "This is your dream come true. You've got a great host family that lives in a wonderful house, you already speak French like a native, and you're bound to have the time of your life while you're here. But don't forget that this isn't my dream! To me, this is a . . . a nightmare."

"It'll get better," Kristy said reassuringly. "I just know it will."

"It will if you'll help me out," Jennifer said. "Look, you two are supposed to be my best friends, right? So what's the big deal about asking you to spend some time with me while we're here?"

Nina hesitated. "It's just that this is our big chance to live in Paris and, well, we want to get as much out of it as we possibly can. Kristy and I are both eager to meet a lot of people and practice our French and learn about what life is really like here in Paris. . . ."

"Oh, I get it," Jennifer said loftily. "So you don't have any time for a boring old American like me. Is that it?"

"No, Jen, that's not it at all." Nina's voice was gentle.

But Kristy stood up, her fists clenched in frustration. "In a way, that's exactly true," she said angrily. "Just because you're miserable doesn't mean you have a right to drag us down with you."

"Thanks a lot!" Jennifer countered. "Boy, it sure is nice to know who your friends are."

"If you were a real friend, you wouldn't be asking us to hold your hand the whole time you're in Paris. We're here to live like natives, not to pal around with whiny Americans who can't even manage to have a good time when it's handed to them on a plate!"

"Oh, so that's what you think of me?"

"That's how I think you're acting."

"Come on, you two," Nina said. "Kristy, sit down. Jennifer, stop shouting. Look, Jen, of course Kristy and I will spend time with you while we're all here. I mean, we're together right now, aren't we?" She cast Kristy a meaningful look. "But I think Kristy has a point when she says that it's important for us not to cling to one another too tightly. If we're afraid of taking some chances, of going out on our own a little, we're not going to get as much as we could out of our stay in Paris."

"That *is* what I meant," Kristy said apologetically. "Look, Jen, I didn't mean to jump all over you. It's just that . . . well, I'm really thrilled to be here. And I can't wait to start learning my way around this city, acting like this independent world traveler, doing stuff I've never had a chance to do before. . . ."

Her voice trailed off as she spent a moment thinking about what some of those things might be—especially one in particular, something she had given a lot of thought to. "Anyway, of course we're here for you. Just not every single second of the day, okay?"

Jennifer wasn't sure whether she should feel reassured or rejected. Nina, meanwhile, wasn't about to give her the chance to spend too much time worrying about it.

"Now, enough of sitting around, yakking away," she said, standing up and pulling them both to their feet. "I don't know if you two have noticed, but right now we happen to be in one of the most magnificent art museums in the world. Let's cover it head to foot, okay? Did you know this used to be a train station, and it was converted into a museum just a few years ago? It certainly looks like a train station. . . ."

And she was off, playing tour guide. Kristy was only too happy to follow along, taking in the artwork surrounding her and hanging on to Nina's every word. But Jennifer remained quiet, still not certain of what to make of all this.

Yes, it was making her feel better to be with her two best friends. It was even kind of fun, in a way. The only problem was, she wasn't completely convinced that she would be able to count on Nina and Kristy to get her through the summer.

3

THE BUILDINGS, STREETS, AND COURT-
yards that comprised the campus of the Sorbonne,
Paris's fine university located on the city's colorful
Left Bank, made up a complicated maze that was
certain to confuse even the brightest new student.
At least, that was what Kristy concluded as she
wandered around, on the edge of panic as she tried
to find the location of her first class.

"Now let's see," she muttered. "If room thir-
teen was over there, then shouldn't room twenty-
three be right above it, upstairs . . . ?"

It was the first day of classes, and like all the
other students participating in the Project for International Exchange, Kristy had intended to de-
scend upon the university campus a bit early, at
least ten minutes before nine o'clock, the time at
which the first of her three morning classes was
to begin. But she had gotten lost on the subway,
and by the time she reached the correct building,
she had only minutes to spare.

She had hoped she would be able to follow the
crowd. But she quickly remembered that the doz-
ens of students who were in the program did not
necessarily have the same schedule. In fact, it was
set up so that three different groups of students
rotated through three different classrooms—one for

French language, one for French history, one for French culture. Kristy was on her own, trying to find Room 23. All the other students, it seemed, had already found their way. Now, with only two minutes left before her first class was about to begin, it looked as if she hadn't much hope of arriving on time.

She was totally exasperated, almost at her wits' end, when she heard someone ask in French, speaking in a kind voice, "Excuse me, Mademoiselle, but are you lost?"

She whirled around, partly embarrassed at having been caught, partly relieved that it looked as if she were about to be rescued. Standing there behind her, looking amused, was a boy who was as handsome as a movie star. He had blond hair, green eyes, and a big smile.

"Uh, I, uh . . ." For the moment, every word of French she had ever learned completely flew out of her mind.

"Ah. You are American." The boy's smile widened. "In that case," he went on, switching to English, "I will take advantage of that fact to practice speaking English." He frowned. "I am doing okay? You can understand me?"

"I can understand you just fine," Kristy replied hastily, having already turned her attention back to the problem at hand. "What I can't understand is this stupid building."

"Stupid?" the boy repeated, looking bewildered. And then a look of recognition slowly crossed his face. "Oh, yes. Stupid. Not very intelligent, am I right?"

"Yes, you're right. Just tell me one thing. Where is room twenty-three? I'm about to be late for my

very first class. Oh, dear, if only I hadn't gotten so
lost on the subway—I mean, the métro—coming
over!''

"Do not look so . . . so . . .'' The boy searched
for the correct word for a few seconds, then
shrugged. "Come. Follow me.'' He couldn't help
adding, "That is correct? 'Follow me?' ''

"Excellent,'' Kristy said impatiently, following
him down the hall. "I only wish my French were
one sixteenth as good as your English.''

"Here you are,'' the boy announced triumphantly about ten seconds later. "It is here, this
room twenty-three.''

"Here?'' Kristy frowned. She could have sworn
she passed this room about eight times already,
yet she didn't remember having seen a number
"23'' on the door. "Okay, then. Thanks.''

With that, she hurried inside, barely paying attention as she heard the boy behind her, calling,
"Okay! Good-bye! Have a nice day!''

In fact, she forgot all about the boy as she sat
through her first three hours of class. It was actually *fun*, she was surprised to discover. Taking
classes here was different from any school she had
ever been to.

In her French language class, for example, she
found that she had new motivation when it came
to listening to the teacher. After all, she had realized that she was going to have to become fluent
in French if she really wanted to experience Paris
like a native. Instead of merely memorizing verbs
or trying desperately to remember vocabulary
words for an upcoming quiz, she knew that this
time around it was for real.

And her teacher, Monsieur Gautier, seemed

very much aware of this fact. He started out by reviewing simple but useful phrases. "Which subway should I take to get to the Sorbonne?" they rehearsed in unison. Then came, "I'd like a hamburger, French fries, and a chocolate milkshake." Then he moved on to more difficult ones. She was also surprised by how quickly she was mastering even slang, now that she had a real use for it.

The next hour of class was spent listening to a lecture, given in English, about France's history. While she had expected that to be dry, instead she found their teacher an engaging speaker. Already he was making the city come even more alive as he talked about how it had been built and what had actually happened here. It was more like hearing a story than studying.

Much to Kristy's surprise, her third class turned out to be the most interesting. She had expected that studying French culture would involve learning about the art and the music. Much to her delight, however, she discovered that it also included lessons in French customs and manners. Kristy recognized that it would be helpful to know the correct way to behave in certain situations. Finding out how to get a taxi, for example, or being told that it wasn't necessary to tip a waiter because a service charge was always automatically added on to the bill, were valuable lessons.

As she filed out of her third and last class of the morning with the other students, she heard a familiar voice calling to her.

"Kristy! Kristy! Over here!"

She turned and saw Jennifer, grinning at her and waving energetically.

"Oh, hi, Jennifer." She headed over in her direction. "So how did you enjoy the first day?"

Jennifer shrugged. "Oh, you know. It was just as boring as I expected."

"Boring! Are you kidding? I thought it was fabulous! I mean, I feel I learned more French in an hour with Monsieur Gautier than in six years of studying at Weston High. And all that stuff about getting around in Paris . . . don't you think that's useful?"

Jennifer made a face. "I suppose. Hey, listen, how about getting some lunch? There are a bunch of cafés around here, but I'm still shy about ordering in French." She chuckled self-consciously. "You know me."

"Jennifer," Kristy scolded. "You've got to start some time. Otherwise you'll starve by the time the summer is over. Besides, it's fun, speaking French to French people. It's like . . . oh, I don't know, like speaking some crazy, made-up language and then finding out that people really understand what you're saying."

"They'd never understand me," Jennifer grumbled. "My French is terrible. Come on, Kristy. Take me to lunch with you."

"Excuse me, but I thought we had made planes for lunch," a male voice suddenly interrupted.

"Planes?" Jennifer repeated. "What are you doing, going to the airport with this guy?"

Instead of being offended, the young man who had helped Kristy find the right classroom laughed. "I have made a mistake, no?"

Jennifer looked at him oddly. To Kristy, in a voice that was only slightly softer than usual, she said, "I wonder if this guy knows the word 'weird.'"

Instead of siding with Jennifer, Kristy found herself growing angry. This boy had been so nice to her, going out of his way to help her—even going so far as to help her out in their communication by speaking English—and Jennifer was simply discounting him.

So when he said, "I hope I am not too late to invite you to have lunch with me," Kristy didn't hesitate before answering.

"I would love to have lunch with you," she said. "You can practice your English, and I'll practice my French."

"Hey, wait a minute," Jennifer cried. "Kristy, I thought you were going to have lunch with me!"

"Sorry," Kristy insisted, standing firm. "I think that having lunch with this authentic Parisian would be much more of a learning experience."

"Learning experience?" Jennifer came back. "Kristy Connor, what kind of a friend are you, anyway?"

Kristy just shrugged. "Sorry, Jen. But I came to Paris to learn, and that means meeting the people here. This is my first real chance, except for my host family."

Leaving behind a pouting Jennifer, Kristy walked off with her new French friend.

"*Allons,*" she said to him, not even glancing back. "Let's go!"

"This is so strange," Kristy commented over lunch at a café near the Sorbonne. "You are speaking English, I am speaking French. . . ." She laughed as she popped one of her French fries, or *frites*, into her mouth. "This has got to be the strangest conversation I've ever had in my life!"

"Yes, it is strange," the boy sitting opposite her agreed with a smile. "But it is good practice. Now, I haven't told you my name, and you haven't told me yours. I call myself Alain. . . ."

"My name is Alain," Kristy corrected him automatically.

"Your name is Alain, too?" he asked, baffled. When he saw her chuckling, however, he understood. "Ah. Now I understand." Carefully he said, "My name is Alain."

"And my name is Kristy. Kristy Connor."

Their conversation continued on like this. It was good practice, Kristy realized, and having Alain speak in English, no matter how faulty, did make it pretty easy to understand him.

He was a full-time student at the Sorbonne during the year, she learned, and this summer he was taking an extra class just for fun. His main interest was geology—an interest, he said, that most people simply could not understand. And that included his parents.

As Kristy listened to Alain fill her in on his background, she was having some interesting thoughts of her own.

This boy doesn't know me, she was thinking. He doesn't know anything at all about who I am. And so I could tell him anything . . . and he would just believe me. After all, he would have absolutely no reason *not* to.

It was then that Kristy decided that she was ready to try out a plan that had been smouldering in the back of her mind for a long time now—ever since she had first learned about the school trip to

Paris, in fact. So what if she had never felt as if she were the person she really wanted to be? So what if her younger sister acted in television commercials and Broadway plays and her older sister was picked to be queen of just about everything?

She was in Paris now, where no one knew her. And that meant she could be anyone she wanted— as long as she was willing to stretch the truth a bit.

Alain sat back in his chair and looked at Kristy intently. "So here I have been talking about a minute a mile—"

"You mean a mile a minute."

"Oh, yes. A mile a minute. And I have not given you the chance to say a single word. Tell me all about yourself, Kristy."

"Well, let's see." Kristy took a deep breath. Could she really do it? Even before she insisted to herself that she could, however, she heard a flood of words come out. It was almost as if someone else were saying them.

"I come from one of the wealthiest families in New York," she said loftily. "I don't mean to brag, but my father is the president of a huge corporation. He's very well known in America. He even had his picture on the cover of *Time* magazine."

"*Time* magazine!" Alain seemed impressed. "I have heard of that. There is even a European edition, you know. Perhaps I saw his picture . . . ?"

"Uh, no. I mean, probably not. I, uh, think his picture was only on the cover of the American edition. Anyway, he's very important. And very, very rich."

"I see. And your mother?"

"My mother . . . my mother used to be a famous movie star."

"Really? And what is her name? I love movies."

"Uh, her name is Carolyn Connor."

Alain frowned. "I do not think I know this name."

"She's very famous," Kristy insisted.

"Well, perhaps that name is a little bit familiar. . . . "

Kristy held back the urge to giggle. It was working. Alain was actually buying her story. And now it was time to really let loose. . . . "But my mother isn't the only actress in the family." Kristy paused, her heart pounding wildly. "I've, uh, been in quite a few movies myself."

"You! Really?"

She swallowed hard as she nodded.

There. She had done it. In an instant, Kristy had been elevated from a very ordinary high school girl with a head full of dreams to a star. A star that was capable of outshining both her sisters, a star who could live up to every expectation her mother had ever had for her daughters . . . a star who was someone who really, really mattered. And as reluctant as she was to admit it, she was loving every second.

As she continued to construct her little story in her own mind, she noticed that a man had sat down at the next table. And from what she could tell, he seemed extremely interested in them. He looked like he was trying to listen in on their conversation. She decided she'd better talk a little bit more softly, just in case this man heard her talking about how important she was and started to bother her.

"So you must have a wonderful life back in the United States," Alain was saying, sounding envious. "It sounds as if you and your family have everything. Money, status, fame . . ."

"Yes, I guess we do. And I don't want to show off or anything, but my life is pretty great. I mean, I'm always going to parties—parties full of celebrities and socialites, the kind of thing that gets written up in magazines and newspapers all the time."

"Really?" Alain asked breathlessly. He was obviously impressed.

"Uh, yes. That's right. Anyway, I don't care all that much about my, uh, fans. My family is much more important to me. My parents just adore me, of course, and we spend so much time together. Traveling, going to the theater . . . I have two sisters, you know. One is younger and one is older. But do you know what?"

"No, what?"

Kristy leaned forward and spoke quietly, as if she were confiding in Alain one of her deepest, darkest secrets. "I really think I'm my parents' favorite. I'd never want my sisters to hear that, of course."

"They are here? Here in Paris?" Alain blinked.

"Well, no, but . . ." Kristy shrugged. "Anyway, I was glad to come to Europe for the summer to get out of the public eye. It gets annoying after a while, always having photographers and reporters following me wherever I go. Magazines are always calling me to ask me to model, movie producers constantly come by the house—uh, one of our houses, I mean, since we own two . . . I mean, three—to ask me to star in their pictures."

She glanced over at the man, who was still staring. She wished he would just go away. But she decided he was just somebody nosy—perhaps someone who was mystified by the strange conversation that was half in French, half in English—and she tried to ignore him.

"I'm really just a simple girl, when you come right down to it," she told Alain, waving her hands in the air. "You know, I don't care about all the fuss that everyone always makes over me. It's just not important to me."

"Hmmmm. Yes, I can see that that might get to be a real . . . what is the word? 'Pull?' "

"What? Oh, I think you mean 'drag.' Yes, Alain, it can get to be a real drag."

Just then, the man came over to their table. But instead of speaking to her, as she had expected, he addressed Alain. He spoke in a low voice, so quickly that Kristy couldn't make out what he was saying. She caught a few words and phrases, but nothing that would let her make any sense out of his animated conversation.

Alain, meanwhile, simply shook his head.

"No, no," he said, turning away. "Not today."

The man finally went away, looking crestfallen.

"What was that all about?" she asked.

"Oh, nothing. That man just wanted some money. He was . . . what is the word? Ah. A beggar."

"Goodness! He was so well dressed!"

Alain smiled. "This is Paris, remember?" He took a pair of sunglasses out of his pocket and slipped them on. Kristy glanced up at the sky in confusion. She hadn't noticed that it was getting any brighter.

Alain, noticing her puzzlement, commented, "I get these terrible headaches sometimes. My eyes are very sensitive."

"If you're not feeling well, Alain, perhaps you should get some rest. I could accompany you home on the métro, if you like."

"Oh, no, no. That is all right. Thank you, but I . . . I have some errands I must do."

Kristy smiled. "This was fun," she said sincerely. "I really enjoyed having lunch with you today."

"Well, then, we must do it again soon. How about tomorrow?"

With a laugh, she said, "I'd love that, Alain." Shyly, she added, "I've really enjoyed talking with you."

Alain frowned. "Kristy, before we go any further, there is something I feel I must tell you."

"What, Alain?"

"I . . . I am not like you. I am not from a wealthy family. My father, he runs a small store on the outskirts of Paris. My mother, she is happiest when she is just sitting by herself, daydreaming, lost in her own little world. We are just ordinary people, not like you at all."

"Oh, Alain!" Kristy cried. "I don't care about that. I . . . I like you just the way you are." She smiled at him flirtatiously. "So, lunch tomorrow, right?"

"Lunch tomorrow." Alain returned with a grin, looking relieved. "Kristy Connor, you are a date!"

When Kristy returned to the LeBlancs' house later that afternoon, she was overcome with a mixture of emotions. What a day it had been. First, her exciting courses, opening up a whole new world to her. Then, meeting Alain. She liked him very much, and she was already looking forward to seeing him again.

But superimposed over her joy over all the good things that had happened to her that day, there was her uncertainty about what she had told Alain. All those stories about how famous she was. Then there were the things she had said about how important her parents were, how much they adored her, how she was so much in demand socially . . . why, she had made it sound as if she were the hottest thing around.

Part of her wanted to toss her head and say, For goodness sake, what Alain doesn't know won't hurt him. This is my chance to fly . . . to be somebody *important*.

But another part of her felt bad for having fibbed—especially to someone as nice, someone as trusting, as Alain. Now she would never really know if he liked her . . . or if he liked who he thought she was.

Her worrying about all that was put aside, however, as she was greeted by Madame LeBlanc, her host "mother."

"Ah, Kristy, there you are," the woman greeted her in French, wearing a big, friendly smile. "Your classes were good?"

"Very good. I'm already learning so much. Today I learned how to yell at a taxi driver who tried to cheat me on the change."

Madame LeBlanc laughed. "That will be very helpful during your stay here, I am sure! Kristy, a package came for you today. It is from the United States."

"A package? Oh, boy! It's probably from my parents."

"I left it on your bed. Don't be long, though. Dinner will be ready in less than half an hour."

"*Merci*, Madame LeBlanc." Already Kristy was hurrying to her bedroom, anxious to see what her parents had sent her.

Sure enough, there was a cube-shaped box sitting on her bed, wrapped in brown paper and string. And it was, indeed, from her parents. Kristy ripped open the box, trying to guess what it could possibly be.

It turned out to be the last thing she would have expected.

"A camera?" she cried, disappointed. "And it's not even one of those automatic ones, the kind that's so easy to use."

With a frown, she took it out of the box and examined it. It was, from the looks of it, an expensive camera, one that came with all kinds of attachments and lenses and a whole book of instructions. There was also a note inside the box.

"Hope the pictures you take will help you remember your summer," it said.

"Boy, I'm surprised they even noticed I'm gone," she mumbled. "But then again, maybe this is their way of saying they're glad that I'm out of their hair."

Then she sighed. "What on *earth* am I going to do with such a fancy camera?" she wondered out loud.

But having nothing else to do in the half hour before dinner, she sat down on the bed, the camera's manual in her hands, determined to make some sense out of all the lenses and buttons and settings.

No one would ever have guessed that the pretty, dark-haired girl hurrying down the street was secretly pretending she was someone else. As she made her way down one of the narrow back streets of Paris, she was, in her imagination, another young woman, one who was about the same age, one who was experiencing the same excitement over being in Paris.

This is the day I've been waiting for for years, thought Nina. These are the same streets that my grandmother walked. This is exactly how she felt.

For the moment, at least, she felt as if she knew her grandmother better than she ever had before.

Nina reached into her pocket for the hundredth time that day. Yes, it was still there. The bundle she had brought with her across the ocean, the one that, up until just a few days ago, she had kept stashed away at the bottom of Anna Wentworth's trunk. She wanted to make sure that the packet of letters, tied together in tattered pink ribbon, was safe.

They were love letters, written to her grandmother fifty years earlier by a man named Marcel du Lac. But they were even more than that. They were also clues, clues to a mystery that for more than five decades had gone unsolved, at least for a young man who at one time had been very much in love with a beautiful woman shrouded in secrets. . . . And written on the front of each one of those letters in a careful, controlled handwriting was the same address: Number 7, rue des Fleurs.

When she finally spotted the blue sign printed

in white letters with the same street name—rue des Fleurs, street of flowers—Nina's heart leaped. She had found it. She was finally here. She began walking more quickly, scanning the numbers on the buildings she passed.

She was growing uneasy, however. Instead of the quaint houses she had expected to find, the small tumbledown cottages with flowers planted in front, the way she had been picturing all along, there were office buildings here. Modern office buildings.

Nina frowned. Perhaps there was some mistake.

But she remained optimistic as she eagerly sought out the number on each of the buildings she passed. Twenty-eight, twenty-one, fourteen . . . and then she found herself standing in front of Number 7.

"Oh, no!" she cried aloud. Her heart, instead of pounding wildly with excitement, suddenly felt as if it had dropped into her stomach.

Number 7 rue des Fleurs, the address that should have been the charming home of an old man named Marcel du Lac, was a brand-new medical center.

Nina just stood in front of it for what seemed a very long time. Could this be the end *already*? she was thinking. Was this really the conclusion to a mission she had planned for ages, something she hadn't been able to stop thinking about ever since she had first heard of the possibility of coming to Paris this summer? An overwhelming wave of disappointment floated over her as she thought, Have I dreamed about this moment for so long, only to have my little exploration end before it has even begun?

At the same time she realized that she had been more than a little foolish. Did you really expect that Marcel du Lac, the man in Grandmother's letters, would still be sitting in the same house he was living in more than fifty years ago? she asked herself crossly. Did you think he would be standing in the doorway, waiting for Anna Wentworth's granddaughter to come strolling around the bend?

Nina thought about turning around and going back home. After all, that would have been the sensible thing to do. To forget all about this silly plan, to admit that she had been thinking like some romantic dreamer . . . But somehow, the idea of admitting total defeat was simply too much to bear. Suddenly, acting entirely on impulse, Nina found herself heading into the building.

Inside, the lobby of this spanking new clinic was clean and efficient. It was decorated entirely in black and white, giving the impression that this was a no-nonsense place.

Nina went up to the stylishly dressed receptionist sitting just inside the clinic's front door. *"Pardonnez-moi,"* she said in her almost perfect French. "Excuse me. I am looking for someone who lived at Number seven rue des Fleurs. A man. An older man."

"Is he a patient here?" The receptionist did not seem very interested.

"No, no. Let me explain." Nina took a deep breath. It was harder communicating in French than she had ever expected—at least when she was trying to talk about something that was so important to her. "A long time ago, a man named Marcel du Lac lived at this address, right here where this building is. . . ."

The receptionist stared at her blankly.

"Here. See for yourself." Nina reached into her skirt pocket and drew out a letter. "See? Monsieur Marcel du Lac, Nombre sept rue des Fleurs."

"*Qu'est-ce que c'est?*" the woman asked, shaking her head in confusion. "What is this?"

"Many years ago, a man lived here. He . . . oh, never mind."

Suddenly, Nina's mission seemed impossible. Her treasure hunt for the past—for her grandmother's past—had met up with a dead end.

"Thank you. *Merci,*" she said lamely.

As she turned away and started toward the door, she was overcome with disappointment. Her dream of finding Marcel du Lac, a dream she had held on to for so long, was suddenly gone.

She had just pushed open the glass door to leave when she heard someone cry, "*Mademoiselle, attendez!* Miss, wait!"

Even though she was certain that she had simply been hearing things, Nina glanced over her shoulder. Hurrying toward her was a tall, slender woman wearing a white lab coat over an attractive deep blue dress. There was a stethoscope around her neck. The woman's dark eyes were bright, and her cheeks were flushed.

"*Oui?*" Nina said. "Yes?"

"Mademoiselle, I heard you asking about a man who used to live at this address."

"Yes . . ." Nina's heart was pounding.

"Maybe I can help you. You see, I am a doctor on staff here. I was a member of the board of directors of this clinic when we bought the rights to this land."

Nina's eyes widened. "Do you remember the

houses that were here before . . . and the people who lived in them?"

"Yes. At least I think I do. It was seven years ago. I was on the committee that talked to the people who owned the houses here. We helped them find new places to live before their homes were replaced by this new building." The woman's expression softened as she added, "I know that seven years probably sounds like a very long time to you, but to me it is not such a long time."

Nina pulled out the letters. "Monsieur du Lac? Do you remember him?"

The doctor frowned as she thought for a few seconds. Then, all of a sudden, her face lit up. "An older man? In his seventies? With very blue eyes, eyes as blue as the sea?"

Nina laughed. "Yes, that sounds like it could be him. At least, according to these letters. Tell me, do you remember where he went?"

The doctor's smile faded. "No. I am afraid not."

Forcing a smile, Nina said, "Thank you anyway."

"Wait one moment." The woman's eyes grew narrow. "This Monsieur du Lac. Did he like flowers?"

"Yes! At least, I think so. At one time he gave a bouquet of yellow roses to a special woman, a woman he was in love with, every single day."

"Hmmm. I remember talking about yellow roses to an old man right after the land sale went through. And I seem to remember him saying he wanted to take the money he was getting from the sale of his house here in Paris and use it to buy a house in one of the small towns to the south of Paris. He said that now that he was leaving the house he had lived in his whole life, the very first thing he was going to do was plant a flower garden."

"A small town . . . in the south?" Nina's mind was clicking away. "Could you please tell me the names of some of those towns?"

"Yes, of course." The doctor spoke slowly, giving Nina a chance to jot the names down on the pad of paper she had in her purse. "You might try looking him up in the telephone books for those towns."

"Telephone books. That's a wonderful idea!"

It was all Nina could do not to lean over and give the doctor a hug.

4

"I GUESS I SHOULD TRY USING THIS THING," Kristy said to Alain, opening up her tote bag and taking out the camera her parents had sent her. "I've read the manual cover to cover, but this is the first time I've actually brought it out of the house. The truth of the matter is that I'm a little bit afraid of it."

"Ah, this camera has teeth?" Alain joked.

Kristy laughed. And it wasn't only because of Alain's sense of humor. She was excited about being on her first real date with him. After an entire week of meeting her for lunch right after her morning's classes, he had invited her to a movie on this cool Friday evening. They had met at the Arc de Triomphe, the tremendous arch built by Napoleon at the beginning of the nineteenth century in honor of his victorious army.

"Well, then, if you're ready to give that camera a try, why don't you take my picture?" Alain offered.

He struck a few amusing poses as Kristy clicked away. It was fun, she discovered, trying different settings, attempting different effects. He was a willing model, but she quickly grew bored.

"I think I'll take some artsy shots," she decided.

"Something like that bench over there. Or maybe this sewer cover."

Alain rolled his eyes upward. "Oh, no. Already the Parisian artistic spirit is getting to you."

After she had used up an entire roll of film, the two of them decided to go off in search of a movie. The Arc, located in the middle of La Place de l'É- toile, was at the edge of the Champs-Élysées, one of the city's best-known boulevards. While it had at one time been a street lined with elegant shops, it was now little more than a crowded tourist mecca.

Aside from the shops and cafés that catered to the city's visitors, there were many movie theaters on the strip. Kristy was disappointed to see that most of them were featuring American movies, either dubbed into French or accompanied by French subtitles. As she and Alain strolled down the Champs-Élysées, enjoying the view of all the people passing by, they read the marquees of the theaters.

"Your choice," Alain said. "We have Sylvester Stallone, Clint Eastwood, Jane Fonda, Sally Field—"

Kristy shook her head. "No, Alain. I'm in France. I want to see something French. Let's find a movie I couldn't see at home in the States."

"I don't know if you would enjoy something like that."

"Sure I would. Besides, I want to learn everything I can about French culture. And what better way is there than actually experiencing it first-hand?"

They continued their wanderings until they stumbled across a much smaller theater, tucked away on a side street. Kristy probably wouldn't even have noticed it if she hadn't been looking so hard, determined to find exactly what she was looking for.

"There!" she announced triumphantly. *"Night of a Thousand Moons.* Let's see that."

She went over to the theater and studied the movie posters displayed out front. She had never heard of any of the actors in the movie. The star, from what she could tell, was a beautiful woman with thick black hair named Charlotte LePage. And according to the poster, she was France's number-one actress.

"This is the movie I want to see," she told Alain, who had come up behind her.

"But Kristy," Alain protested. "I don't think you will like this movie very much. It's so . . . so French."

"That's the whole idea!"

"But I read some of the reviews, and it's supposed to be terrible."

"I don't care." Kristy shrugged. "I want to see it anyway."

"But this theater is always so . . . so *hot* inside."

Kristy was growing impatient. "Alain," she said, "you told me I should choose any movie I wanted to see, and this is the one I am choosing. Now are you coming along, or should I go by myself?"

"You American girls," he muttered, grinning despite himself. "Once you make up your minds about something, there is no holding you back."

"I don't understand," she said a few minutes later as she and Alain sat inside the theater, waiting for the film to begin. "If this movie got such bad reviews, why is the theater so crowded? We're lucky we even got seats!"

"Oh, well, it is Friday night. All the movies are crowded on the weekend."

"And it's interesting that even though it is so crowded, this theater isn't hot at all. In fact, I'm quite comfortable."

Alain just shrugged. "Maybe they fixed their cooling system." As if he were trying to change the subject, he commented, "I suppose you go to the movies all the time."

"Huh? What do you mean?"

Alain was grinning. "Kristy! You *are* a famous movie star, don't forget!"

"Oh, right. Uh, sure. I go all the time."

"How about opening nights? Are they exciting? Tell me what they're like!"

"Oh, well . . . Really, Alain, no words can describe them. . . . Gee, it is getting a little warm in here, after all."

"What kind of movies do you make? Have I ever seen any of them, do you think?"

"Oh, probably not," Kristy replied with a wave of her hand. "I don't think any of them have ever been released in Europe. It, uh, has something to do with licensing. I signed a contract once that made it impossible for . . . Oh, look. The movie is starting."

Kristy was relieved that the lights were finally going out. Talking about her stardom—her *made-up* stardom—made her uncomfortable. She still wasn't sure if she had made a mistake in making up all those stories in the first place, especially since she was becoming so fond of Alain.

But this was no time for worrying about that.

She was quickly drawn into the movie. It had a clever, involving plot, and Kristy's French was good enough for her to follow it—and even to understand some of the more humorous lines.

But what struck her most was its mesmerizing star. Charlotte LePage was a beautiful woman and a wonderful actress. It was easy for Kristy to understand how she had become the country's most popular movie actress. By the end of the film, Kristy was ready to sign up for her fan club herself.

"What a fantastic movie!" she cried as she and Alain walked out of the theater.

"I guess the critics don't always know what they're talking about," Alain said with a rueful smile.

"That Charlotte LePage is wonderful. I'd love to find out more about her."

"Really? Why?"

"Oh, I don't know. I was just really struck by her talent and her beauty." She eyed him curiously. "Why, don't you like her?"

Alain laughed. "Kristy, all of France loves Charlotte LePage. Why should I be any different?

"Now enough about movies," he said firmly. "How about something more real? Something like my stomach. I'm hungry, and I happen to know a place that makes the most wonderful chocolate éclairs in Paris."

Kristy was only too happy to say yes.

"Gee, Kristy. I'm really thrilled for you," Jennifer said dryly. "It sounds like you've met the man of your dreams."

"Well, I wouldn't go that far," Kristy replied

uneasily. She could tell from her friend's tone of voice that she had made a mistake in calling her up to report on her date with Alain.

You should have known how she was going to react, Kristy told herself. She made a vow that, from then on, she would be careful about what she told her friend.

Jennifer, meanwhile, was in a terrible mood when she hung up the phone.

Great, just great, she was thinking. Everybody is having the time of their lives except me. She started to retreat to her bedroom, armed with the latest book she had bought, a novel written in English. Well, I've managed to get through the first week, anyway. Only seven left to go.

On her way to her room, however, she met up with Madame Cartier. She was wearing a huge smile, as always.

"Ah, Jennifer, there you are," the woman said in French. "I have some good news for you."

I can only imagine, Jennifer thought. "What is it?"

"I have invited my granddaughter, Michèle, up to Paris for a while. She lives in Lyons, but she often comes to stay with Henri and me. She loves Paris so, and of course we always enjoy seeing each other."

Terrific. Another Cartier to deal with. "When is she coming?"

"In a few days. And I am certain you will like her, Jennifer. She is seventeen years old, about the same age as you. And she is so much fun." Earnestly Madame Cartier added, "I think she will help you have a better time while you are here in Paris."

But I don't *want* to have a good time in Paris, Jennifer was thinking. All I want to do is get this summer over with—and have as little to do with anything or anybody as possible.

And when she finally managed to get away from her talkative hostess, she went into her bedroom, closed her door, and began writing one of her daily letters to Danny, in which she repeated exactly that.

What a different world the small town of Sainte Marie was from Paris. As Nina stepped off the train, she could hardly believe she had traveled only ten miles south of the bustling city. The sweet air, the sound of birds singing, and the quiet streets, practically deserted so early on a Saturday morning, were her first real reminder that there was more to France than the cosmopolitan city she had already begun to think of as home.

She was pleased that she was getting the opportunity to see a charming little town like Sainte Marie. But as she set off toward the center of town, she reminded herself that she was hardly here on a sight-seeing trip. Her research into the telephone books for the region south of Paris, the suggestion of the kind doctor at the clinic at Number 7 rue des Fleurs, had told her that there was only one Marcel du Lac. This morning, Nina intended to find him.

Slowly, the town was beginning to come to life. As she walked down the main street, the shops were just opening. The proprietor of a tiny flower shop was arranging bouquets of bright, colorful blossoms. Up ahead, the owner of the grocery store waved to her before turning the metal crank

that opened up the red-and-white striped awning.
Already she was getting a warm feeling from the
people who lived here.

Yes, Sainte Marie was special, a picture post-
card come to life. It was precisely the kind of place
in which she would expect Marcel du Lac to be
living.

"Pardon, Monsieur," Nina said, approaching the
grocer. He was a heavyset man in an apron. He
had gotten the awning in place, and now he was
patiently unpacking a huge basket of peaches and
arranging them on a wooden counter underneath
the awning.

She showed him the address she had carefully
printed on a piece of paper, wanting to make certain she did not make any mistakes. The man nodded, pointing and letting forth with a spew of
sentences. He spoke so quickly that Nina didn't
catch everything he said. But she understood
enough.

What an adventure this is turning out to be, she
thought. On an impulse, she stopped and bought
a small bouquet of flowers. Clutching it tightly in
her hand, she continued on, still relishing the feeling of the early morning sun on her back, the
sweet sound of the birds chirping, the peaceful
sight of this small French town getting ready for
the new day.

When she found herself standing in front of the
house whose address matched the listing she had
found in the telephone book, Nina was certain this
had to be the right place. The house was small but
carefully kept. It was white with pale blue shutters that looked as if they had just been painted.
As she peeked around the corner, Nina saw that

in the back there was an exquisite garden, a lush growth of vibrant flowers in every color of the rainbow.

And in the front, there were no fewer than six rosebushes. And every one of them was bursting with bright yellow blossoms.

Nina laughed. This simply had to be the right place.

Suddenly her smile faded. What if Marcel du Lac wasn't here? She hadn't even considered that possibility up until now. She had been so determined to find him, so excited over finally having the chance to talk to him, that she had never even entertained the idea that he might not be in. He could have gone away for the summer, he could have moved to a new house . . . there were a hundred different possibilities.

Suddenly she could wait no more. Nina opened the gate and strode through the tiny front garden, crossing in just a few short steps. Her heart was pounding as she knocked loudly on the wooden door.

"Please, *please* be home," she muttered. "And *please* be the right Marcel du Lac!"

The moment the old man opened the door, Nina knew she had found him. His eyes perfectly matched the description her grandmother had given in her letters. They were warm and lively . . . and the color of the sky on a cloudless June morning.

"Monsieur du Lac?" Nina asked breathlessly.

"*Oui*," the man said, nodding his head and looking a bit confused.

"Marcel du Lac?"

"*Oui, c'est moi.*" Yes, that's me.

Nina took a deep breath, then spoke in slow, careful French to make sure he would understand.

"Monsieur," she said, "my name is Nina Shaw. I am the granddaughter of Anna Wentworth."

"When I heard you say her name," Marcel du Lac said in a voice hoarse with emotion, "that was the first time I have heard anyone speak of her in almost fifty years. I thought my heart would stop beating."

Nina and Marcel were in the small living room, sitting next to the front window that looked out on the rosebushes. The shutters were open, and as a breeze wafted in, it caused the yellowing lace tablecloth thrown over a rickety table to flutter. On it was the tea Marcel had made, served in delicate china cups. He had also brought out a loaf of dark brown bread and a small piece of cheese. But so far, neither of them had touched the food.

"And Anna, you say, has been gone now for . . . for how many years?"

"Almost four," Nina replied. "I miss her terribly."

Marcel leaned forward in his old wooden chair, his blue eyes narrowing as he peered at Nina. "Ah, yes. I can see it. I can see Anna in your face. The same nose, the same eyes . . . but mostly I see that same smile. Yes, you are very pretty."

"Am I as pretty as my grandmother?" Nina asked teasingly, unable to resist.

The old man thought only for a fraction of a second before answering. "Ah, I am afraid that no one could ever be as pretty as your grandmother."

He stood up and made his way across the room, stopping at the chest of drawers that was pushed into one corner. The top was covered with old photographs, most of them black-and-white. He opened the top drawer, reached underneath the assortment of things stashed inside, and pulled out one more photograph.

"Here she is," he said, his voice almost reverent. "I have saved this for all these years."

He brought the photograph over to Nina and presented it to her like a fine gift. Then he stood back, his eyes still on the picture. It was a photograph of her grandmother—not as Nina remembered her, but as a beautiful young woman, probably not much older than Nina was now. Her eyes were shining, and a flirtatious smile played about her lips. In her slender hands she was holding a bouquet of roses, blossoms so full they looked ready to burst with life.

It wasn't hard to tell from the expression on the young woman's face that she had very strong feelings about whoever was taking that photograph.

"I took that picture in Paris," Marcel said, answering her question before Nina had a chance to ask it. His voice was filled with excitement. "It was just after we met." He paused, then asked, "Do you know the story of how we met?"

"I do know it," Nina returned with a shy smile, "But I would like very much to hear you tell it."

"Ah, it was so very long ago. I was a student in Paris, studying law. I was a lawyer for many years, you know. I practiced in Paris.

"I still remember that day as if it were only last week. I was hurrying off to class. I was late, as usual. I was running down the Boulevard St. Germaine, on the Left Bank, near the Sorbonne. I was trying to get to class on time, really I was. But all of a sudden I noticed a beautiful young woman, carrying a big art portfolio, standing on the corner. There was a flower shop there, and she had stopped to lean over and sniff a bouquet of yellow roses that was outside the shop.

"When I saw her, I stopped. It was as if I had been struck by lightning. I knew I had to meet that girl, and suddenly nothing else mattered. Certainly not getting to class on time!"

Marcel du Lac laughed. For a moment, all the stress, all the signs of age, left his face. For that fleeting second, Nina was able to see him as he had looked fifty years earlier—as he had looked when he was a young man, about to fall in love with her grandmother.

"I went over to her, bold as could be, and said, 'Ah, Mademoiselle. Do you like flowers?' "

He laughed, then shrugged his shoulders. "And that was how it began. After a meeting like that, how could Anna help but fall in love with a charmer like me?"

His cheeks turned pink as he asked, "Did she ever tell you that she and I were very much in love?"

Nina nodded. "Yes. She told me everything. Or, to be more exact, the letters told me everything."

"The letters?" Marcel looked confused.

She reached into her purse and pulled out the stack of letters she had found in her grandmother's trunk, more than twenty of them, lovingly tied together with a piece of faded, fraying pink satin ribbon.

"Do you remember these?" she asked gently, holding the stack of paper out toward him.

Marcel remained silent but his eyes filled with tears.

"Oh, my," he finally said. "My letters. She saved them."

"Yes. Your letters to her, and letters from friends she had written to about you and the feelings the two of you had for each other. She kept them in a special place where no one would ever find them. And she held on to them her whole life." Nina took a deep breath. "I felt greatly honored that when she died, she left me an entire trunk filled with her most personal and beloved things. There were wonderful old clothes inside, hats with feathers and beautiful dresses and some jewelry I know Grandmother had loved . . . and at the very bottom, tucked away where they would not be easily noticed, I found these."

Marcel sat down and took the stack of letters that Nina was still holding out to him. Lovingly he untied the ribbon, keeping his eyes away from Nina. He took out the first letter, opened it up, and read it. Nina could see the emotion that registered in his face.

"Ah. You have read these?"

"Yes. Every one."

"And so you know the whole story."

"I know what happened in Paris fifty years ago," Nina said gently. "As for the 'whole story . . .' Well, that is why I wanted so much to come speak to you. I wanted to tell you what happened. I wanted to tell you my grandmother's side of the story, something you haven't known up until now."

The man sat back in his chair. "I am ready to listen."

Nina took a deep breath. "Monsieur, the reason I know so much about this is that in addition to the letters, my grandmother also left me her diaries. One of them was the journal she kept the year she spent in Paris—and the months that followed, when she came back home to the United States."

"Go on."

"I know how it looked. The two of you were so much in love, and then, one day, she just left without any explanation. She never even said good-bye. You wrote to her for months, but you never got any reply. Finally, you just gave up."

"Yes," Marcel said softly. "That is what happened."

"My grandmother knew that you thought she left because she didn't love you enough to stay. Or perhaps that you decided she hadn't loved you at all, that she was merely toying with you while she was in Paris."

Marcel nodded slightly. "That did occur to me," he said sadly. "But I never believed it. Not really."

"Monsieur, let me explain. My grandmother had very strict parents. And in those days, young women always did what was expected of them. Yes, she was allowed to come to Paris for a year to study art and polish her French and learn a little bit about life. That, in those days, was acceptable. What was *not* acceptable was for a nineteen-year-old woman to break away and do what she wanted instead of what her parents had decided was best for her."

"And what did Anna's parents think was best for her?"

"To come back home and marry a successful and respectable man who would make her a good husband. Someone who would provide her with security and take care of her her whole life."

"I understand," Marcel said. He spoke so softly that Nina could hardly hear him. "And is that how Anna's life turned out?"

"Well, according to her diaries—and according to the things I remember her saying even when I was a small child—the man she married did provide her with security. That man—my grandfather—was a good, solid, loving husband. He was always kind to her and she, in turn, made him a good wife."

"Ah. So it was for the best." Marcel sounded very sad.

Nina bit her lip, trying to regain her composure before speaking.

"Monsieur," she said in a strained voice, "I think it is important that you know that every spring, my grandmother spent hours caring for her garden, a garden filled entirely with yellow roses. And that every summer, she spent her evenings sitting among them, just thinking. Her eyes would take on this dreamy, faraway expression, even when she was very old. All of us knew not to disturb Grandmother when she was sitting among her roses. It was simply understood."

The look that crossed his face made Nina fear that he was going to start to cry. Instead, Monsieur du Lac stood up.

"You must excuse me," he said, stumbling toward the bedroom. "I must . . . I must . . . excuse me."

Nina was afraid that she, too, would start crying

as she watched the old man stumble across the room, hunched over from both age and emotion. She understood that he wanted to be alone. And so she stayed in her chair, only too happy to give him a few moments to himself.

After he had closed himself up in the bedroom, however, she realized that by now the tea he had made for them was cold. The cups needed to be put away and the cheese and the bread needed to be wrapped up. So she stood up and piled all the dishes onto the tray Monsieur du Lac had used to carry them out from the kitchen, then took them into the next room.

The kitchen was charming. Despite the strong emotions that were rushing over her, she couldn't help noticing the delightful kitchen table made of rough-hewn wood, the old-fashioned cast-iron stove, the oversized porcelain sink. The tiles on the wall were hand-painted, perhaps even made in one of the provinces surrounding this quaint town.

A bouquet of freshly cut yellow roses was lying by the sink. Nina realized that when she had knocked on Monsieur du Lac's door, he must have been about to put them in the vase she saw standing on the kitchen table.

After depositing the dishes in the sink and putting away the other things, Nina set about the task of putting the flowers in water. She tore off some of the larger leaves, then looked around for a place in which to dispose of them. Finding none, she headed toward the back door, the bouquet still in hand, having decided to toss the leaves outside.

Once she was in the tiny back garden, she gasped. The garden was beautiful, even more so than she had realized. It was planted with bright, colorful flowers that grew everywhere, rather than in neat, regular rows. Through the happy confusion there was a tiny path made of stones. Surrounding the yard was a rickety old wooden fence.

One bush in particular caught Nina's eye. It was covered with bright red flowers, a variety she had never seen before. In the bright morning sunlight, they were simply irresistible. Still clutching the bouquet of yellow roses, Nina leaned forward to sniff them.

But she jumped when she heard someone say, *"Ah, Mademoiselle, vous aimez les fleurs?"* Ah, Miss. Do you like the flowers?

Quickly Nina stood upright, suddenly embarrassed. She hadn't known she was being watched.

She glanced around, confused about where the voice had come from. And then, on the other side of the fence, over in the next yard, she saw a very good-looking young man, smiling at her. He had straight, dark hair and a gaunt, handsome face, with a sharp nose and pronounced cheekbones. He was tall and lanky without being at all awkward.

What was most noticeable about him, however, was his eyes. They were bright blue and full of life. Nina immediately thought of Marcel.

And when the young man said, in French, "Are you a friend of my grandfather's?" Nina knew right away who he had to be.

"Yes, I am his friend," she replied in French.

"Good. I would hate to think that pretty young women had begun sneaking into his garden to steal his flowers when I was out."

"These flowers certainly are beautiful. Your grandfather is quite a gardener."

The young man came through the gate and into the backyard. He looked at Nina more closely.

"You are not French, are you?"

Nina laughed. "I suppose I should take that as a compliment. Most Americans have such terrible accents that Frenchmen know where they are from right away."

"American? You are American?"

Nina couldn't help smiling over his astonishment. "Is that good or bad?"

"It is just a surprise. I did not know my grandfather knew any Americans."

Now it was Nina's turn to be surprised. She could only conclude that Marcel du Lac had kept his love affair with her grandmother a secret for all these years.

"I do not know your grandfather very well. In fact, we just met today."

"Ah. That explains it. Are you a tourist here?"

"Yes and no. I'm spending the summer living with a lovely couple in Paris. I'm taking language and history courses at the Sorbonne."

"That explains why your French is so excellent. But I am afraid it still does not tell me why you and my grandfather have suddenly become friends."

Nina was about to launch into a long explanation when Monsieur du Lac appeared at the back door.

"Ah, Pierre. You have returned. You brought the milk?"

"The milk, the stamps, the bread, the newspaper . . . everything you requested, Grandpapa." Winking at Nina, he added, "Ah, this old man works me so hard."

"Yes, but there are some rewards," Marcel was quick to say. "For example, you are getting the chance to meet my new friend. Nina, this is Pierre du Lac, my overworked grandson."

Nina laughed, then extended her hand toward Pierre. "My name is Nina Shaw, if I may introduce myself properly."

"Shaking hands!" Pierre pretended to be annoyed. He folded his arms across his chest and shook his head. "Here in France it is much more common to kiss than to shake hands."

"I don't know if it is more common," Monsieur du Lac interjected, "but it is certainly nicer. Especially if the person the young man is meeting happens to be a pretty young woman."

Nina noticed that Pierre's cheeks turned just a tiny bit pink. But Marcel du Lac had already moved on to another topic.

"When I was inside, I had a wonderful idea," he said cheerfully. Nina could see he was back in top form once again. "Since Nina is our guest, and she has never been here in Sainte Marie before, let us take her out to the countryside on a picnic. Since you and I never did get around to having tea," he went on, turning to her, "I would think lunch sounded like a fine idea."

"It does sound like a fine idea," Nina was quick to agree. "But there is one condition. You must let me help pack up the food. After all, I am the one who dropped in on you, uninvited and unexpected."

She was only teasing, but Monsieur du Lac came over to her and took hold of both her hands. His blue eyes were earnest as he said, "Nina, I hope you understand how much it means to me that you have come to us. I think . . . I think you must know."

Nina just nodded. Her throat was suddenly too thick with emotion for her to speak.

Less than half an hour later, Marcel, Pierre, and Nina were piled into a dilapidated old car. It was a convertible, and on a perfect July day like this one, it only made sense that the top would be down.

Pierre drove, and Nina sat beside him. Marcel sat in back, clutching a straw sun hat and hugging the huge picnic basket that rested on the seat beside him. Folded across the top of the basket was a flowered tablecloth, giant pink cabbage roses against a pale green background. It was the perfect touch for an outing in the French countryside.

"Now we will show you the real France," Pierre told Nina. "Paris is wonderful, of course. But this is the most beautiful part. The trees, the fields, the sky . . . the inspiration for the great painters of our country." Glancing over at her, he asked, "Do you like painting?"

"Oh, yes! Especially the works of the Impressionists. Claude Monet, Paul Cézanne, Mary Cassatt . . ."

"Mary Cassatt!" Pierre protested. "But she was an American."

"True, but she painted here in France, and she was friends with all the other great Impressionist painters." Nina sighed. "I could look at those paintings forever."

"Ah. Then you have visited the Musée d'Orsay in Paris?"

"Only briefly with some American friends. I do

want to go back, and I will, the very first opportunity I get. It is just that I have been so busy that I haven't yet made the time."

They had driven for less than fifteen minutes when Pierre pulled the car over to the side of the road. To the right stretched a large field, covered with colorful wildflowers. Beyond was a wooded area, green and fresh and cool. The sun was high in the sky, without being too hot. The only sounds were those of birds chirping and leaves occasionally moving in the breeze.

"Oh, Pierre. This is breathtaking," Nina cried. "How beautiful."

"Yes. In fact, I was just thinking the same thing myself."

She glanced over at him and saw that he was looking at her, not the landscape. She could feel her cheeks turning pink, and she was glad when she heard Monsieur du Lac cry, "Are you young people going to help this old man with this heavy picnic basket, or are you going to spend the whole day chattering away like magpies?"

"Once again, my grandfather is making me work," Pierre said with a smile. He went back to the car to help the old man out and to carry the heavy basket.

Lunch was delightful. Bread and cheese, a bottle of wine and a bottle of mineral water, some peaches and grapes, and, for dessert, an apple tart. Nina stretched out on the edge of the flowered cloth after having eaten her fill, enjoying lying in the sun. She never expected to doze off, but when she jerked awake at the harsh sound of a crow's distinctive *caw, caw,* she realized that her morn-

ing's journey—and the adventure that had followed—had tired her out.

She sat up quickly. Monsieur du Lac was nowhere in sight, but Pierre was sitting at her side,
looking at her and smiling.

"What time is it?" she asked, feeling a little
guilty for having abandoned her kind hosts, even
if only because of a little catnap.

"Don't worry; you were only asleep for a few
minutes."

"I didn't mean to be rude."

"Not at all. I enjoyed watching you. My grandfather went for a walk. He had had enough sun,
and he was looking for a patch of shade so he could
take his own nap."

"So we left you all alone," Nina teased.

"I didn't mind a bit. It gave me a good chance
to look at you." By way of explanation, he continued, "You see, I am studying to be a painter myself. It is summer vacation for me now, and so I
am spending it in Sainte Marie, helping out my
grandfather a bit. During the year, I am a student
in Paris. And so I am always keeping an eye out
for possible subjects to paint."

Nina could feel her face reddening—both with
pleasure and with self-consciousness—at what she
knew was about to come.

"I would love the opportunity to paint you," he
went on casually. "Or, if you do not have the time,
then at least to make a few sketches of you."

"What would you call your painting of me?"
Nina asked teasingly. " 'An American in Paris?' "

"That, I cannot tell until I have finished the
painting. Then you are saying yes, that you will
let me paint you?"

Nina hesitated. "When would we find the time . . . and where would we meet?"

"I will come to Paris, of course. I keep a small studio there. It is where I do my painting. So what do you think? Will you do it? . . . Please?"

Nina lowered her eyes. She knew that the answer to what seemed like a very simple question could, in the end, turn out to be very complicated. She had come to Paris to study, to learn, and to have fun. To agree to Pierre's proposal meant taking a risk. After all, getting involved with a charming young Frenchman had never been part of her plan.

But it was so difficult to keep that in mind as she looked at Pierre, sitting so close to her on the flowered tablecloth, his blue eyes fixed on her with an intensity that made her feel something she had never felt before.

"Pierre," she said in a soft voice, "you are welcome to paint me any time you please."

And as he nodded in agreement, neither of them felt the slightest bit of surprise over the arrangement they had just made. It was as if they had sensed, ever since the first moment they laid eyes on each other, that this was not going to be the last time they saw each other.

5

"THIS WAS SUCH A WONDERFUL IDEA," MAdame Cartier exclaimed in French. "Jennifer, I am only sorry that Henri and I didn't think of it sooner."

Jennifer forced a weak smile. Her reaction, she knew, was not at all what the Cartiers had been hoping for. But somehow, the idea of their seventeen-year-old granddaughter arriving on the scene in order to provide her with instant friendship just didn't excite her.

She'll probably be really stuck up, she was thinking as she sat on a bench at Paris's Gare de Lyon, waiting for Michèle's train to arrive. Or else she'll totally ignore me. After all, this was the girl's grandparents' idea, not hers. Good old Michèle probably doesn't want to be here in Paris, looking after me, any more than I want her here.

But deep down, Jennifer couldn't help being a little bit optimistic. Her own friends, after all, had been such a disappointment. Nina and Kristy were just too busy to spend much time with her. And what hurt the most was that it wasn't just Kristy's new boyfriend Alain or Nina's mysterious quest, the one that had her running practically all over the country, that was getting in the way. No, the two of them had decided that they were only in-

terested in Paris and Parisians. Things like loyalty
and friendship, it seemed, had been left at home.

"Ah, there she is," Madame Cartier suddenly
said, interrupting Jennifer's thoughts. "Michèle!
Michèle!"

The old woman stood up and waved her arms
in the air. Her face was lit up with excitement.
Jennifer, meanwhile, scanned the crowd that was
rushing through the train station.

"Grandmama! Grandpapa!" A pretty, dark-
haired young woman ran up and threw her arms
around the Cartiers, hugging each one of them before stepping back, blinking. "Let me look at you,"
she said in French. "It has been . . . how long?"

"Too long," Madame Cartier replied. "Ah,
Michèle, you look so lovely."

Jennifer had to admit that the girl standing there
with bright blue eyes and flushed cheeks was
pretty. She was also energetic and animated, one
of those people whose faces reflected everything
they were thinking.

"We are forgetting the most important thing!"
Monsieur Cartier exclaimed. "Michèle, you must
meet our guest from the United States. Jennifer,
Michèle, I hope this is the beginning of a fine
friendship."

Jennifer opened her mouth, intending to say
something polite. But Michèle beat her to the
punch.

"Oh, Jennifer, I'm so glad to meet you!" she
cried in English. "I'm so looking forward to having the chance to show you around Paris. I mean
the Paris I love—young people's Paris—not the
stodgy city full of monuments and boring tour
guides that is all that most visitors get to see. And

you don't mind if we speak English, do you? I would really welcome the chance to practice on a real American."

Jennifer was taken aback by the girl's enthusiasm. "Uh, sure, Michèle. Speaking English would be fine. In fact, speaking English would be great. I was afraid I was forgetting how."

Michèle laughed. "Ah, Jennifer. I can hardly wait to begin. I have so many people I want you to meet, so many places I want to show you. I think we are going to have fun, you and me."

Jennifer just stared at her. Was that really possible? Would she really have fun with this girl?

I really, really doubt that, she was thinking, still sizing up her brand-new companion. Then again, I suppose I could at least give it a try. . . .

"You're only posing for a drawing." Nina gazed at her reflection in the mirror, her hairbrush poised midair. "You've never done anything like this before. That's the only reason you have all these butterflies in your stomach."

For the fifth time that morning, she decided to rearrange her hairstyle. Impatiently she pulled out the barrette she had just fastened in back and held it on one side of her head, studying the effect. And then she began brushing her hair fiercely, having concluded that she should wear it loose, with no barrette at all.

"Usually you're so . . . so *level-headed*," she scolded herself. Yet she continued studying the girl in the mirror, casting her a disapproving frown and picking up the rose-colored blush she had already applied twice. "You've always had so much common sense. Yet ever since Pierre called to say he was coming to Paris to do some sketches of you, you've been fussing like . . . like someone about to go off on her very first date.

"Besides," she went on, "the main reason you're interested in seeing Pierre du Lac again is because you want to find out more about his grandfather."

Despite her protests, however, Nina knew she was only fooling herself. The truth was that the idea of seeing Pierre again was filling her with excitement. And both being the subject of his sketches and learning more about his grandfather were only a very, very small part of it.

"You are certainly looking lovely today," Pierre greeted her when they met near the main entrance of the Bois de Boulogne, the huge park on the edge of the city. "You look radiant, as if you were glowing."

Nina laughed. "That's because I was rushing to get here on time. I ran all the way from the métro." But she kept her face down so he wouldn't see the flush of delight on her cheeks.

Pierre's studio was close to the Bois, a short walk through quiet streets lined with well-kept homes. As they walked to the fifth floor of a narrow stone building, up to a large, airy space bright with sunlight streaming through the glass ceiling, Nina suddenly felt shy.

"I've never done this before," she said. "I don't know how I'll feel about having someone stare at me so closely."

"Just keep in mind that I will be breaking you down into colors and planes and shapes." Pierre was only half teasing. "I'll barely see you as a person at all!"

"How's this?" She wasted no time before arranging herself in a comfortable position on the wooden platform.

Pierre studied her for a few seconds. "No, not quite."

He came over to her and knelt down at her side. Touching her lightly, he positioned her face, then gently pulled her shoulders a bit forward, meanwhile frowning in concentration.

"You're treating me like a vase of flowers." Nina pretended to be annoyed. "Or even a bowl of fruit."

"Ah, I told you so. Now keep still, *ma petite*. It is important that the light be just right. It is not a simple matter for an artist to pose his subject."

As he brushed her hair back over her shoulder, Nina felt a shiver run down her spine. Perhaps, in Pierre's mind, all he was doing was rearranging the subject he was about to draw. But to Nina, being so close to him, feeling his gentle touch, was making her feel a rush of emotions she was reluctant to be experiencing.

In fact, as she sat as still as she could, she was unable to stop thinking about how being so near to Pierre had made her feel. Keeping her body motionless, she watched his blue eyes travel from the sketchbook to her face, back and forth, so regularly that it was as if he were watching a tennis match. The scratchy sound of the charcoal against the coarse paper was the only sound that broke the silence of the room.

"Can I see it?" she finally asked, knowing that no more than ten minutes had passed.

"Be patient," Pierre mumbled. "Great art takes time."

She held out for what seemed like an eternity but was probably only another ten minutes. "Pierre, I'm getting tired. It's hard, sitting so still."

"Please, Nina. I'm doing your mouth right now."

After five more minutes had passed, Nina said, "There's something I've been wondering about."

"What is that?" Pierre never changed his expression, never altered the steady back-and-forth movement of his eyes.

"I was wondering about the woman your grandfather married."

"Ah. Grandmother." His handsome face tensed into a pensive frown. He stopped sketching, but his eyes remained glued to the paper. "She and grandfather were not a very good match, I am afraid."

"Really?" Nina's face registered her surprise.

"Nina! Do not move!" Pierre cried, having noticed her change of expression. "How can you expect to be the subject of a beautiful drawing if you keep moving your face?"

"How can you expect me *not* to react when you tell me something like that? What do you mean, your grandmother and your grandfather weren't a very good match?"

"Nina, do you want to talk or pose?"

"Do you really want to know?"

Pierre sighed and put down his piece of charcoal. His fingers were covered with black smudges.

"Perhaps we have done enough for now," he said. "I must admit that you have been a very patient model. We both need a break. And to show you that this temperamental artist is not such a terrible person, I will take you out to lunch and tell you all about my grandparents and their marriage."

Sitting outside in front of a sidewalk café, opposite Pierre at a tiny round table, Nina realized that whenever she had fantasized about what it would be like to be in Paris, this was precisely the scene that she had imagined. The Café des Papillons—"The Butterflies"—was tiny, with red-and-white checkered cloth tablecloths on its dozen or so round tables. The curtains on the windows were made of lace. Even the proprietor of the café was exactly what she would have expected. He was short and chubby with a black mustache, round red cheeks, and a warm, wide smile.

On the sidewalk, Nina could see all of Paris passing by. Fascinated, she watched the parade of people strolling by: women so fashionably dressed they looked as if they had just stepped out of the pages of a magazine; intense young students in jeans engaged in earnest conversations; businessmen and -women hurrying by on their way to a meeting or in search of a quick lunch.

As for the young man with whom she was sitting, the two of them so close that they were almost touching . . . well, Nina had to admit that he was part of her dream, too. But as much as she delighted in his company, she was still not sure what to make of her relationship with Pierre.

He was charming, handsome, and fun to be with. On those points, she was perfectly clear. And it was similarly clear that he liked her. But something was getting in the way of allowing her simply to sit back and let whatever may happen to happen. She was holding back, afraid of admitting her true feelings, feelings that seemed to be growing stronger with each passing minute. But despite her desire to keep her emotions in check, she still had the feeling that she was heading in a direction that was going to make things very, very complicated.

At the moment, however, she was not about to let herself be distracted by either the charm of her surroundings or the charm of her luncheon companion.

"Go on, Pierre," she said impatiently, right after she had ordered a sandwich on a baguette, the long loaf of crusty bread that had already become her passion. "Tell me about your grandmother."

"Ah, yes. *Grandmère.*" He was wearing a devilish grin as he added, "And here I've been hoping you would rather talk about the romance of the city—or the delights of having lunch with me."

Nina laughed. "I'm not saying that Paris isn't wonderful. And I'm not saying that my lunch companion isn't . . . well, let's just say that he isn't without a certain charm." Suddenly she grew serious. "But I really am eager to hear about your grandparents' marriage. Your grandfather is such a sweet man. For years I've wanted to know more about him. This is my chance."

Pierre was silent while their waiter, the plump proprietor of the café, poured them each a glass of mineral water. When he began speaking again, his tone was serious.

"Nina, it is a very sad story. One that my father told me many times." He drew in a deep breath. "After your grandmother left Paris, disappearing without giving a reason or even saying good-bye, my grandfather, Marcel, was heartbroken. For a long time he simply threw himself into his work. He became very successful at his law practice, but everyone could see that he was very lonely.

"Then a young actress came into his life. She was beautiful, they say, and the pictures I have seen of her bear that out. But she was much younger than he was—and, I have heard, after little more besides his money." Pierre sighed sadly. "They were married for a short time, only a year or two. During that time, my father was born. Then, when Papa was just a baby, the woman simply disappeared."

"Disappeared?" Nina blinked. She was so fascinated by Pierre's story that she didn't even notice when the café's owner set her lunch down on the table before her. "What do you mean, she disappeared? Where did she go?"

Pierre frowned. "They say she ran off with a road company, some theatrical group. The man who ran it apparently offered her the lead role in a play that was about to tour Europe. She went off . . . and was never heard from again."

"And your grandfather?" Nina asked softly. "How did he react to all this?"

"Of course he was heartbroken. At least, he was at first. It didn't take him long to realize that it was probably for the best. Yes, he made a few efforts to find her, but he soon gave up. He discovered that whatever feelings he had at one time felt for her quickly faded.

"But his child—my father—was a completely different story. It seems that Grandfather doted on him from the very start. He hired a nanny to care for him when he was a baby, but he devoted every spare moment he had to his son." Pierre shrugged.

"Then my father grew up, got married, and had two sons of his own, me and my brother. And here we are." With that, he reached for his own lunch and began to eat.

Nina, however, was still too enthralled by the story Pierre had just told her to care about anything as mundane as food. "So your grandfather never remarried," she said wistfully. "He was hurt twice, and he gave up."

"It is tragic, isn't it?" Pierre agreed. He spoke slowly as he went on, as if he were being very careful to choose just the right words. "Nina, after you left his house, my grandfather and I had a very long talk. He told me about your grandmother, and how he was destroyed by their parting. It is true that having met you, having heard what really happened, has helped him.

"But the fact remains that many years ago, two people who were deeply in love were separated by forces beyond their control. And my grandfather has never quite recovered from that."

"I don't think my grandmother ever did, either." Nina was picturing her as a very old woman, sitting in her garden, that lost, faraway look in her eyes as she lovingly tended her yellow roses.

She was silent for a long time, lost in her own thoughts. When she finally glanced up, she saw that Pierre was staring at her. There was a strange look in his piercing blue eyes.

"Nina," he said, his voice hoarse, "there is something I have to say. I . . . I am a bit confused right now. I find I am experiencing feelings I have never had before. I have this sense that you and I are heading toward something—"

"Pardon, Mademoiselle," the café's owner suddenly interrupted, coming over to their table. "Is there something wrong with your sandwich? You haven't touched it."

Nina glanced up at him. The concern she saw in the man's face immediately drew her out of her dreaminess. The intense moment that had existed between her and Pierre had vanished. When she looked at him, she saw that he was looking down, suddenly shy.

"Oh, no, Monsieur. The sandwich is fine," Nina was quick to assure him. "We were just so busy talking."

As they ate their lunch, Nina and Pierre talked about meaningless things: the bad traffic on the streets of Paris, the possibility of a spell of hot weather, the differences between living in America and in France. But Nina could not forget the look she had seen in Pierre's eyes. Even more important, she could not ignore the way that being with him made her feel.

"Taking a walk was a lovely idea, Pierre. And I appreciate your agreeing to act as my tour guide, showing me around this section of the city. But it's starting to look as if we might get rained out."

Nervously Nina glanced at the sky. What had begun as a beautiful July day was now clouding over. The temperature was dropping, and from somewhere far in the distance came the rumble of thunder.

"Do you want to head back?" Pierre asked. "The studio is only a few blocks away from here. We could probably beat the rain, if we hurried."

"No, I don't want to go in yet, not until we really have to." With a sigh, she added, "I love this city so much that I want to enjoy it every second I can. I adore walking around. Oh, I know it sounds silly, but with every street I turn onto, every building I pass, I can't help wondering whether my grandmother saw that same building or walked down that same street when she was here."

"I think we're going to have to cut our walk short," Pierre suddenly cried. "It's starting to pour. Here, let's duck into this doorway."

They raced toward the closest shelter, the entryway to a bookstore. And they reached it just in time. Nina and Pierre stood huddled together, gazing out at the sheeting downpour that had seemingly come out of nowhere. He pulled off the light cotton sweater he had been wearing and draped it gently over her shoulders.

"Just look. It's like . . . it's like an Impressionist painting." Nina's voice was almost a whisper. "How lovely the city looks in the rain. I wonder if my grandmother ever stood in a doorway on a day like this, looking out at the gray city. . . ."

"Nina, you are so serious," Pierre interrupted. "You are so concerned with your grandmother, but what about *you*?"

"Me?" Nina turned to face him, blinking. "What about me?"

"What happened between your grandmother and my grandfather happened a long, long time ago. It is part of the past."

"Yes, but . . ."

Pierre's voice sounded oddly husky as he said, "And what about the present?"

"What *about* the present?" Nina asked, not understanding the point he was trying to make.

"The present," he said, "belongs to you and me."

With that, he placed his finger under Nina's chin and drew her face upward toward his. And then his lips were upon hers, kissing her lightly, almost as if he were asking her a question.

Nina was surprised at how urgently she kissed him back. For the moment, all of Paris vanished. The rain, the gray buildings . . . she was aware of none of it. For the moment, only Pierre existed.

All of a sudden, the romance of the city, the promise that seemed to hang in the air, had been realized.

6

"OH, MY GOSH," KRISTY CRIED.

She had just opened the envelope containing her newly developed photographs, the very first roll of pictures she had taken with the camera her parents had sent. She hadn't been expecting anything beyond the usual mishmash of snapshots: Alain in his silly poses, of course, but also some pretentious-looking close-ups of flowers and benches and rocks, all of them out of focus and either under-exposed or overexposed.

Instead, she was pleasantly surprised.

"Wow," she muttered, standing on the street corner in front of the photography shop. "I may not know much about photography, but from what I can tell, these aren't half bad."

"Half bad? On the contrary." A familiar male voice interrupted her. "If anything, I would say these are half good."

Kristy looked up, chuckling.

"Alain, you have a real knack for the English language."

"Knack? What is this 'knack'?" As usual, he was frowning in confusion over the new expression that had just been thrown his way. Kristy was as charmed as always.

But Alain had already forgotten all about trying

to make sense of the strange word he had just heard for the first time. He was absorbed in her photographs. Carefully he examined each one of them, growing more and more excited.

"Kristy," he finally said in an awed voice, "these photographs of yours are magnificent. Why, I had no idea you were such a talented photographer."

"Neither did I," she replied. Rather than being falsely modest, her words were sincere. "I mean, I've never taken any pictures like this before. Oh, sure, I fooled around with one of those Instamatics, taking pictures of my friends or my family or whatever. But this is the first time I ever tried to do anything out of the ordinary. Anything that—you know—tried to make a statement."

"Well, then, you should be especially proud of yourself. In fact, I just had an idea. How would you like to spend your second date with me going to some galleries over on the Left Bank? I happen to know a few that specialize in photography. You might enjoy learning about some of the techniques other photographers use. It could be quite useful."

Kristy was quick to agree. "Who knows? Maybe the work of those other photographers will inspire me. I've already decided to get some more film. In fact, I think I'll go back into that photography store right now. I can use the money my parents just sent me for my birthday."

"Your birthday? I did not know it was your birthday!"

"Well, it's not. At least, not yet. My parents sent me a card a little early. I guess they were being cautious, since the mail has so far to go and all."

"When is your birthday?"

"Next Monday. July twenty-eighth."

"Well, then, I hope you will allow me to take you out to dinner on that evening."

"Oh, Alain, you don't have to do that." Despite her polite protests, however, Kristy couldn't have been more pleased.

"But I *want* to. Of course, the restaurant where I take you to dinner probably won't be as fancy as most of the places you're used to."

Kristy could feel herself blushing. "Really, Alain. Any restaurant would be just fine." She really meant it. In fact, she was tempted, for just a moment, to tell him the truth. She had to admit that it was kind of fun, pretending she was this made-up person who, deep down, she really longed to be. Even so, every time Alain brought up the "differences" that supposedly existed between them—those of social status, wealth, and life-style—she doubted more and more whether or not her clever little idea of inventing an entirely new identity for herself had been such a good one, after all.

At the moment, however, she was too excited to worry about it. She was thrilled about Alain's invitation to a birthday dinner . . . and she was equally thrilled over having discovered that she had a talent for photography.

"Well, then, let's check out those galleries," she said to Alain.

And in an uncharacteristically brave action, she looped her arm through his. Maybe the real Kristy Connor, the one who was a social zero, wouldn't have had the self-confidence to try something like that. But when it came to the *other* Kristy Connor, the successful, self-confident girl who had everything, throwing caution to the wind was almost second nature. That Kristy, after all, was completely comfortable with the notion of getting *exactly* what she wanted—especially if that meant having the time of her life romping around Paris with a boy she really liked.

Jennifer, meanwhile, was finding that her days in Paris had become even more tiresome, now that she had become the charge of an overly enthusiastic tour guide. The Cartiers' granddaughter Michèle was determined to show her a good time. In good weather and bad, she dragged her out of bed early, outlined the day ahead over breakfast, and then tore around the city until nightfall, keeping her reluctant sidekick informed with her cheerful, nonstop chatter.

"Tonight I want to take you to a club," Michèle said, pulling Jennifer off the métro at a stop on the Left Bank. "It's a great place with really loud music. There's one band I particularly like. All the musicians have striped hair."

"Striped?"

"But right now I want to show you an exhibit by the number-one photographer in France. This gallery has an exclusive show of the work of Robert Moulin. Do you know his work?"

What could be more boring than photographs? Jennifer was thinking as she followed Michèle into the tiny gallery, a rundown, out-of-the-way storefront that was nevertheless mobbed. I'll probably end up looking at pictures of the guy's vacation.

Much to her surprise, however, the photographs on display were unlike anything she had ever seen before. At first glance, the huge black-and-white blowups were undistinguishable. They looked like nothing more than designs, odd collections of shapes and colors. But as she looked at them more closely, she saw that they were actually photographs of everyday items like paper clips, ice cubes, and soap bubbles.

"Well, Jennifer, what do you think?"

"Frankly," Jennifer replied without a moment's hesitation, "I think they're awful. I've never seen anything so strange in my whole life."

"Awful?" Michèle's confusion was apparent from the expression on her face. "Am I understanding the English correctly? You don't like them?"

"I hate them. Can I make it any clearer than that?"

"But Robert Moulin is one of the most famous, most successful photographers in France! He is considered a genius. Here in Paris, everyone is talking about him."

"There you have it." With a toss of her head, Jennifer folded her arms across her chest. "It just goes to show you that there's a basic incompatibility between the French and the Americans. It's a cultural difference. We don't see eye to eye on anything, and we never will—"

"They really are magnificent, aren't they?" In the next room, someone else was speaking English—with a very definite American accent. "What a wonderful eye this Robert Moulin has. What an imagination. . . . Jennifer, is that you?"

Jennifer was astonished to find herself face-to-face with Kristy.

"Kristy! What are you doing here?"

"I was just going to ask you the exact same question! This is great, Jen, running into you like this. . . ."

All of a sudden, the smile on Kristy's face faded. "Uh, I, uh—"

"Are you here alone?" Jennifer was looking around the gallery.

"Uh, yes. I mean, uh, no." Kristy froze. The last thing in the world she wanted was the chance for Alain to have a long conversation with one of her American friends, someone who knew the real Kristy Connor. All it would take was one slip, and the truth would come out. And as Kristy grew more and more fond of Alain, the prospect of having him find out that she was a fraud grew even worse.

"Well, Kristy, are you alone or not? That's not exactly a trick question."

"Uh, I'm with Alain. You know, that boy from the Sorbonne."

"Oh, yes. Him." Jennifer made a face.

Kristy, meanwhile, was glancing nervously over her shoulder. She was lucky; at the moment, Alain was so wrapped up in one particular photograph that he hadn't even noticed she had run into someone she knew.

"Look, Jen. This guy is pretty shy. I'd rather you didn't—"

"Shy! You've got to be kidding! Just about every time I see him, he's pushing his way into our conversation."

"This is different. He and I are on a date and, uh, I don't want anything to go wrong. *Please*, Jen!"

Jennifer just shrugged. "Gosh, Kristy, are you ashamed of me?" But she turned away.

"Thanks, Jen," Kristy whispered. "I owe you one."

"Was that someone you know?" Michèle asked pleasantly, glancing over at the red-haired girl who was hurrying away.

Jennifer gave her an odd look. "I'm not sure."

The rest of the day was a whirlwind of sightseeing. It was true that the Paris that Michèle was showing Jennifer was not the one that most tourists got to see, Jennifer admitted begrudgingly. She supposed she was lucky to see the boutiques full of wild clothes, the off-beat galleries, the tiny cafés that were hangouts for students and other young Parisians. And when Michèle told her the ice cream parlor she took her to was the best one in all of Paris, she didn't doubt her for a moment.

"So what do you think of Paris now?" Michèle asked with a grin a few hours later as the two girls plopped down into a seat on the métro. They were headed back to the Cartiers' apartment for dinner, tired after a long and busy day. "There's a lot more to it than monuments and museums, isn't there?"

"Yeah, I guess there is." Jennifer let out a loud sigh. "I just wish we didn't have to go back to your grandparents' house."

Michèle was surprised. "You do not like my grandparents?"

"Oh, uh, I didn't mean that, exactly. They're nice and everything. I mean, I can see that they're trying really hard to make my stay here in France as much fun as they can." With a sigh, she said, "They're just not the most exciting people in the world, that's all."

Michèle raised her eyebrows. But before she had a chance to reply, the métro jolted to a stop.

"Hey, this is our stop, isn't it?" Jennifer said, jumping to her feet. "Come on, hurry up. We don't want to end up in nowheresville."

"Nowheresville?" Michèle repeated.

But the frown the French girl was wearing as she followed her American companion off the train was not because of the peculiar new word she had just heard.

"You know," Nina said wistfully, linking her arm in Pierre's, "I've been dreaming about coming to Paris practically my whole life. Ever since I was a little girl, I have been reading books about it and watching movies about it. I've spent a lot of time fantasizing about it, too. Now that I'm here—"

"Now that you're here, you're disappointed?" the handsome young man interrupted with mock seriousness.

"Oh, no. I'm not at all disappointed!" When she glanced over and saw the expression on his face, she realized that he was teasing. Playfully she punched his arm. "I was going to say that now that I'm here, I keep finding myself in situations that are exactly the way I'd always imagined they would be."

"Does this happen to be one of those times?"

"Mmmm."

Nina sighed as she looked around her. She was making a mental list of all the elements that were responsible for her joyous mood. It was a warm, sunny Sunday afternoon, with just the hint of a breeze that kept the July day from becoming too hot. In honor of what seemed a perfect day, she and Pierre had taken a train trip out of the city to the town of Versailles.

The elaborate palace of Versailles had housed four French kings, including Louis XVI and his wife with extravagant taste, Marie Antoinette. The palace was so grand, in fact, that the contrast between the way royalty lived and the way most Frenchmen lived had contributed to the French Revolution.

It was truly an amazing sight. The elegant castle

consisted of several buildings, filled with elaborately decorated rooms. There were acres of gardens, pools, and fountains, and the carefully maintained grounds were dotted with pieces of fine sculpture. It was like something out of a fairy tale, so sumptuous that it was difficult to believe that people had ever actually lived there—even kings and queens.

Today, however, its sense of history was considerably lessened by the fact that it was filled with tourists. In fact, the line to get into the castle wound completely around the huge front courtyard, bigger than a city block. Pierre and Nina weren't the only ones who had come up with the idea of visiting the beautiful and historic castle on a Sunday afternoon like this one, and waiting times for tours were well over an hour.

But they didn't care in the least. They were more than happy to spend the afternoon wandering around the grounds, strolling among the fountains and the manicured gardens and the marble statues. It was so romantic, walking hand in hand along the gravel paths, talking together and enjoying their lush surroundings.

Pierre had brought along a picnic basket, filled with tasty things he had picked up at a *charcuterie* in Nina's neighborhood on his way over to pick her up. They had just finished off a light lunch of cheese and baguettes and apple tarts.

"Aside from taking long strolls around castles with charming Frenchmen who adore you," Pierre went on jokingly, "how are your studies going?"

"Very well. That is, when I have time to study." There was a twinkle in her dark brown eyes as she added, "Between spending time with those charming Frenchmen and posing for their paintings, I'm afraid there isn't much time left for reading about the history of France."

"Ah, but you must make the time. I do not want to distract you from your studies." Pierre's expression had grown serious.

"Actually, I've been doing some writing," Nina said in a voice that was meant to be light.

"Writing? I didn't know you were interested in writing."

She nodded, casting him a shy look. "As a matter of fact, it's what I hope to do as a career."

"Why, that is fantastic, Nina. What type of things do you write?"

"Stories, mostly. But one day . . ." Nina took a deep breath. She was, after all, about to confide something that she had never before said to anyone. "One day, I hope to write books."

"*Magnifique!* Ah, yes, that fits so well. In fact, it is perfect."

"*What* is perfect? What are you talking about?"

"Why, you will be a great writer, I will be a great painter, and together we will be the toast of Paris! We will invite other writers and painters to our home. It will become the artistic center of the city . . . perhaps even all of Europe, and—"

Nina laughed. "My goodness. That's a wonderful fantasy."

But Pierre wasn't laughing. "It doesn't have to be only a fantasy, Nina."

She looked over at him, surprised. She could see how earnest he looked. Even so, she couldn't resist trying to tease him out of it. "Pierre du Lac. This isn't a proposal, is it?"

He just looked back at her with wide eyes.

"Nina," he said, "I know we are too young to get

married. We are both just starting out with our adult lives. I must see how far I can go with my painting. I must develop as an artist, and study and learn. . . . And you have to grow as a person so that you can grow as a writer. I would never think of asking you for a commitment at this point in your life."

He hesitated for a moment before going on. "But I do know one thing," he said, his eyes growing sad. "If I am going to have to stand at the airport in just a few short weeks and watch you get on a plane so you can fly out of my life forever. . . ."

He never finished. Instead, he looked away, staring off into the distance, not willing to complete the thought that had been nagging at them both almost since the day they first met.

"Nina, I owe you an apology," Pierre said later that afternoon.

He and Nina were on the train back to Paris, after spending the entire afternoon at Versailles. Even though they were tired, they were both filled with a sense of euphoria, the feeling that came from having a wonderful time with someone special. They were relaxed, as well, as they sat shoulder to shoulder, glad to be heading back to the city.

"An apology?" Nina repeated, blinking. "For what, Pierre?"

"For the things I said earlier this afternoon." He frowned. "I don't mean to rush you, or to put pressure on you. Believe me, that is the very last thing I would ever want to do."

Nina remained silent, waiting for him to go on.

"It's just that . . ." He turned his face to the window. "Look," he said, his tone suddenly changing. "There it is. Paris. See the buildings up ahead? It is

the most beautiful, most romantic, most wonderful
city in the world. And it belongs totally to us.''

It belongs to *you*, Nina was thinking, but not to
me. She felt a wave of sadness as she reflected on
Pierre's words, meanwhile looking out at the view
that had filled him with such joy.

Yes, there was Paris, its beautiful blue-gray sil-
houette rising up along the horizon. It was like a
jewel. The City of Light, it had been nicknamed.
Seeing it like this—the way it seemed to emerge
from out of nowhere as the train made its way
closer and closer to it, the way it glowed in the
fading light of late afternoon—she finally understood what had inspired that name.

But it was true that while it was Pierre's city, it
was not hers. For the first time in days, she thought
about her own home. How dull life in Connecticut
seemed, compared to living in this European cap-
ital where the streets were filled with vibrant,
passionate people.

How she would miss being a part of all this. Stepping into an art museum and being inches away from
some of the finest masterpieces ever created. Walking up to a stand on a street corner and buying the
flakiest apple tart imaginable, still warm from the
oven. Or turning off a major boulevard and finding
herself on a quaint cobblestone cul-de-sac that made
her wish that, like Pierre, she had a gift for capturing
on canvas what she beheld with her own eyes.

And how uninteresting the people back home
seemed. Especially the boys she had known back
in Weston, boys who cared about little besides
sports and television. How far away all that
seemed to her now . . . and how unsatisfying.

Shyly she sneaked a peek at Pierre. She saw that

he was watching her. Did he sense that she was thinking about him? she wondered. And did he know that she was comparing him to the boys she had known back home . . . and finding that, unsurprisingly, in her eyes there was absolutely no comparison at all?

"Anyway, we should not be talking of such unhappy things like your leaving Paris," Pierre went on with forced cheerfulness. "We must concentrate on what is happening here and now. These are the moments that matter."

When they reached the station in Paris a few minutes later, Nina found that the idea of leaving Pierre and going to the Rousseaus' home for the evening was unbearable. Of course they were lovely people, and she looked forward to telling them all about her day at Versailles. But saying good-bye to Pierre, especially now that she was in such a melancholy mood. . . .

Before she had even made a decision about what she wanted to say to him, she turned and cried, "Pierre, don't go. Not yet. Let's . . . let's have dinner together. I'll just call the Rousseaus to tell them I've made other plans."

She was pleased when he took her to the same café they had visited together the day he made his first sketch of her, the one with the red-and-white checked tablecloths and the plump, mustached owner. He wasn't there on this Sunday evening, but that didn't matter. At the moment, Pierre was the only person Nina was seeing, anyway.

"Pierre," she said hesitantly after their waiter had brought them their dinner, "remember those things you were saying before, about the way it will feel when I have to leave at the end of the summer?'' She swallowed hard. "I have been thinking about that, too."

He nodded. "Nina, what are you going to be doing in the autumn, when you go back home to America?"

"I am going to college."

"You are excited about this?"

Nina shrugged. "Not really. The college I am going to is small and not very far away from where I grew up. I'm afraid it won't be much of a challenge. Things won't be too different from the way they were last year."

Pierre looked surprised. "If you feel that way, then why did you choose such a place?"

"I didn't really choose it," she said slowly, realizing even as she said the words that they sounded absurd. "My parents chose it."

"Your parents. But I do not understand. Why are they the ones to choose where you will study, where you will live . . . how you will be spending the next few years of your life? You are practically a grown woman, Nina. Isn't it time you made such decisions for yourself?"

His expression immediately turned to one of sheepishness. "I'm sorry. There I go again, exploding all over the place, trying to tell you what you should and shouldn't do." He laughed. "So perhaps I am not so different from your parents."

"No, you are right about my making my own decisions," Nina told him. "I know you are. But sometimes . . . sometimes it is simply easier to go along with what other people want for you. Especially if those people happen to be your parents."

"Ah, yes. Sometimes I forget that." He looked sad as he added, "My father died when I was twelve, my mother when I was fifteen. Since then, as you know, I have lived with my grandfather. He is a great influence in my life, of course, but he and I have always just taken it for granted that I would make all those decisions on my own."

"It's not that the college I'm going to is a terrible place or anything," Nina was quick to interject. "It's just that . . ." She sighed. "To tell you the truth, Pierre, before I came to Paris, going to school there seemed to make perfect sense. It was the obvious choice, and it never occurred to me to contradict my parents. But now that I have come here, now that I have lived in this wonderful city. . . ."

"And now that you have met me, of course." Pierre was trying to sound as if he were teasing.

But this time, it was Nina's turn to remain serious. "Yes, that, too," she said. "Having met you has also changed the way I look at things."

She stared at the edge of the tablecloth for a long time, silent. When she finally looked up at him, her eyes were wet.

"Pierre," she said in a voice choked with emotion, "I don't understand what I'm supposed to do. Now that I have met you, now that I have fallen in love with this city, how am I supposed to get on a plane at the end of the summer and fly away? How can anyone expect me to leave behind everything that has become important to me?"

Nina shook her head in confusion. "I know this was supposed to be just a summer trip, a chance for me to learn and to expand my horizons and all that. But it's turning out to be so much more complicated than I ever dreamed. I never expected to feel so much at home here. I'm astounded every time I open my mouth and hear entire French sentences come out. It's as if I had been born to speak this language. Sometimes I even find myself thinking in French.

"And then . . . and then there's you." She paused, swallowing hard. "I . . . I don't understand the way I feel about you, Pierre. I've known you only for a few weeks. It's such a short time; I know it is. But even so, it's as if you're the person I've been waiting to meet my whole life. It's as if I already knew you, somehow, and understood all along that it was just a question of time until I found you." She looked at him pleadingly. "It's such a strange feeling, something I've never experienced before."

"I think I know what you mean," Pierre said, so softly that Nina could hardly hear him. He reached across the table and took her hand, holding it firmly in his. "And I think I know what that feeling is called. It's love, Nina. I know that I love you. And what about you? Do you think perhaps the feeling you are talking about could be love?"

As Nina looked into his deep blue eyes, she felt as if she were falling into them. And at that moment, she understood that the magic between them was special, something that would never fade.

"Yes, Pierre," she said. "I know it is love."

7

"SURPRISE, SURPRISE!" CRIED NINA, THRUST-
ing a box that was carefully wrapped in pink-and-
lavender paper, then topped with a floppy pink
bow, at Kristy.

"Happy birthday," chimed in Jennifer, who was
also holding a gift. "Surprise, Kristy!"

And Kristy really was surprised. The very last
thing she had been anticipating that Monday afternoon as she met her two friends in front of the
library at the Sorbonne—supposedly for a study
session—was an impromptu little birthday celebration.

In fact, she didn't even expect them to have remembered that today was her birthday, what with
all the excitement of being in France for the summer. Sure, she had mentioned it once or twice, just
in passing. But she had had no idea they would do
anything special.

Yet here they were, both of them with presents
in hand. A large, mysterious basket sat on the
bench beside them, covered with a neatly folded
cloth.

"Those are our party refreshments," Nina informed Kristy, noticing where her eyes had traveled.
"We figured it would be much more fun—much

more Parisian—to have a birthday party for you outside in one of the parks."

"I wanted to have it at McDonald's," Jennifer said, laughing. "I thought you might enjoy having a real *American*-style birthday party. But Nina talked me out of it."

"Any place would have been just fine," Kristy assured her friends. She was sincerely touched by their thoughtfulness. "But Nina is right. Having a picnic does seem very Parisian. And the idea of celebrating my eighteenth birthday in Paris is so exciting that I might as well do it in a way that makes me feel French."

And so the three girls set out to find a shady, grassy spot near the Sorbonne, strolling a few blocks over to the famous Jardin du Luxembourg. The grounds surrounding the Palais du Luxembourg, built in the early 1600s, were just the right place for an occasion as important as this one. Kristy, who had already explored this park thoroughly with Alain after one of their lunch dates, led the others to the Fontaine de Medicis, a long, rectangular pool of water surrounded by ornate carvings that was a popular resting place for both Parisians and tourists.

Once they were comfortably seated, Nina lifted off the cloth, spread it out on the lawn, and took out a square white bakery box.

Kristy gasped. "A birthday cake?"

"Well, of course. What did you expect?"

"But where did you ever find a birthday cake . . . in Paris?"

Even Jennifer laughed. "They celebrate birthdays here, too, you know."

Sure enough; inside the box there was a chocolate raspberry *gâteau*. Lying in the box next to it were eighteen candles—plus one for good luck. Even the candles were special. They were very long, almost ten inches, and as thin as toothpicks.

"They're called *bougies*," Nina informed them, arranging them in a circle on top of the cake. Shyly, she added, "Pierre told me about them."

"What a beautiful cake!" Kristy cried. "Here, let me take its picture. I'll take your picture, too."

As she readied the adjustments on the camera she had begun carrying with her at all times, Nina commented, "Goodness, Kristy, you're becoming quite a shutterbug, aren't you?"

"A *what*?" Jennifer said.

Kristy translated for her. "A camera freak." She was wearing a big grin. "Well, yes. I guess you could say that. And the best part, aside from the fact that I'm really finding it fun, is that it turns out I have kind of a knack for taking pictures."

"Oh, no." Jennifer groaned. "Not another Parisian *artiste*!"

Nina and Jennifer had also brought along a bottle of Coke, as well as napkins, paper plates, plastic forks, and plastic knives. They had thought of everything, going to quite a bit of trouble to make Kristy's eighteenth birthday special. When they began to sing "Happy Birthday," it was all she could do to keep from bursting into tears. Instead, she leaned forward and blew out her candles.

"You guys . . ." she said hoarsely. "You're really too much. Both of you."

"I hope you remembered to make your wish," Jennifer reminded her.

"What more could I possibly wish for besides two great friends like you?"

Jennifer looked at Nina and grinned. "Maybe one of the things in these boxes. At least I hope so."

"Open this one first," Nina urged, picking up the pink-and-purple package. "It's from me."

Her gift was a dictionary of French slang expressions. As Kristy unwrapped it, Nina teasingly explained, "It's to help you with your romance with Alain."

"Well, I don't know how much of a *romance* we're having," Kristy returned with a sigh, "but it'll be helpful with whatever is going on between us. Alain is probably the sweetest boy I've ever met in my life, but his English . . . well, let's just say it's a little bit more creative than what I'm used to."

Nina laughed. "Maybe I should have gotten him a dictionary of English slang."

"Hey, what is going on with you guys, anyway?" Jennifer asked. "He waits for you after class every single day. You two are a real item, going out for lunch together like clockwork."

"And I heard that you've been going out in the evenings, too," Nina said. "If all that's not a romance, then I don't know what is."

Kristy smiled. "He *is* taking me out to dinner tonight. He wants to celebrate my birthday in style."

"Oh, cool!" Jennifer leaned forward excitedly. "Where is he taking you? Someplace fancy? One of those fine gourmet restaurants that serve snails and rabbits and stuff like that?"

With a shrug, Kristy said, "I don't really know. You see, I get the impression that Alain comes from a family that doesn't have very much money.

His father runs a shop somewhere on the outskirts of the city."

"You mean like a little grocery store or something?" Jennifer asked.

"I think so. Anyway, I know he would love to take me out to a really special restaurant. I just hate to have him spend a lot of money on me."

Especially since if he did, it would mainly be because he thinks that's the kind of treatment I'm used to, Kristy was thinking. In fact, she was tempted to confess the whole thing to Nina and Jennifer. In the end, however, she realized that she was so embarrassed by the way in which she had lied to Alain that she would never be able to bring herself to admit it, not even to these girls, her two best friends in the entire world.

"Well, Kristy," Nina said, "I hope you're not letting the fact that Alain isn't exactly the number-one playboy of Paris bother you."

"Oh, no! Not at all. In fact . . ." Kristy was aware that her cheeks were turning bright red. "I kind of like him. I mean, like, a lot."

"Oh, terrific," Jennifer groaned. "So you're falling in love with a French boy. That's all you need, to leave him behind in another few weeks. Which reminds me."

She turned her attention to Nina, who had been just about to cut the cake. "How are things with you and Pierre?"

Nina froze, the plastic knife she was holding poised in midair. "Things are . . . wonderful."

Jennifer rolled her eyes upward in exasperation. "Oh, boy. So far, that's two broken hearts out of three. As a group, I'd say that we're not doing very well."

Nina opened her mouth to speak, but then quickly snapped it shut. How could she explain to Jennifer that the feelings she had for Pierre were nothing to joke about? This was serious . . . even more serious than she had been willing to admit to herself. She was glad she could turn back to the distraction of cutting the cake and placing generous slices on the flimsy paper plates.

"Goodness, Jennifer," Kristy was saying, "what a pessimistic attitude you have. What's wrong with all of us enjoying what we have right now? Sometimes I get the feeling you're trying hard *not* to like Paris."

Jennifer shrugged. "I'm just waiting it out, that's all."

"Aren't you having any fun?" Kristy asked.

"Well, this is fun. Hanging out with you guys, I mean."

"What about your host family? You haven't said very much about them."

With a snort, Jennifer said, "Them? They're just two old people who hardly ever go out. What could possibly be more boring?"

Nina handed her a piece of cake. "Didn't you say they invited their granddaughter up to Paris? She lives in Lyon, right?"

"Yeah. Michèle." Jennifer shrugged. "She's okay, I guess. She just tries a little too hard, that's all. I mean, she's been taking me all over Paris, and she has shown me some pretty neat things. I don't know. I guess maybe I'm just one of those people who can't get excited about anything that's so far outside her own experience."

Nina and Kristy exchanged frustrated looks as Jennifer picked up the present that had been resting next to her on the grass. "And speaking of things that are familiar . . . happy birthday! Here, Kristy. This is for you. Open it!"

Kristy was only too happy to do just that. Inside was a stack of magazines . . . all of them *American* magazines. Wrapped up in colorful birthday paper were the August back-to-school issues of *Seventeen*, *Glamour*, and *Sassy*.

"I searched all over town for these," Jennifer explained triumphantly, "but it was worth it. A little taste of home, you know? Plus they'll help you get psyched for going back and starting school in the fall. It's just a few weeks now until Labor Day!"

Once again Kristy and Nina exchanged meaningful looks. Nina, it was clear, was totally frustrated with Jennifer's attitude. But Kristy just laughed.

"Thanks, Jennifer. This is a terrific present. It's so . . . so *you*."

"Why, thank you!" Jennifer seemed really pleased by the compliment.

"Now, how about some of that birthday cake?" Kristy said. "It looks fantastic."

"Just make sure you save some room for tonight's dinner," Nina reminded her. "Don't forget, those snails and rabbits and all those rich French sauces can be pretty filling."

"I know it's probably not the kind of place you're used to," Alain apologized for the tenth time, "but I think you will like this restaurant anyway. The food is quite good, and the atmosphere is fairly quiet."

"Oh, Alain, it's just fine," Kristy reassured him,

also for the tenth time since he had picked her up at her host family's house earlier that evening to take her out for her birthday dinner. "In fact, this place looks wonderful."

It was true that the supposedly "modest" restaurant that Alain had chosen to take her to this evening was, in fact, a cut above the kind of place that Kristy had been expecting. It was called Beauvilliers, and it was located on Montmartre, one of the livelier sections of Paris. Restaurants and cabarets were crammed onto the hill that was topped by Sacré-Coeur, a graceful white church with distinctive architecture.

The restaurant itself was actually made up of several small rooms, the walls painted in rich colors to create an intimate atmosphere. There were huge bouquets of flowers everywhere. And there were so many waiters tending to them that Kristy felt like a queen. Some of them, in fact, treated Alain so well it was almost as if they knew him. There were even snails and rabbit on the menu—although, fortunately for Kristy's somewhat less adventurous taste, it had chicken and fish as well.

"This was such a sweet idea," Kristy commented once she and Alain were seated at a table right near the window, one that afforded them an excellent view of the lovely summer evening sky. "Thank you for inviting me tonight, Alain."

"Well, Kristy, I had to . . . how do you say, make the large deal about your birthday."

Kristy smiled. "I appreciate your 'making a big deal' about my birthday. Some of my American friends had a little party for me this afternoon, too. Oh, nothing special, just a picnic. But I feel lucky to have so many people looking after me."

"You know, I would love to spend time with your American friends," Alain said. With a twinkle in his eyes, he added, "Sometimes I get the feeling you are trying to keep me away from them. Perhaps you are a little bit ashamed of your simple French boyfriend?"

Kristy hesitated. She didn't know whether to feel excited over the fact that Alain had referred to himself as "her boyfriend" or nervous about his interest in meeting her friends. Not that she was embarrassed by him, of course, not at all. What she was was fearful of was that Nina or Jennifer or any of the other kids she knew from Weston High School would spill the beans about her true identity. And given the way she was starting to feel about Alain, that was something she simply could not risk.

Before she could try to explain that she simply had not yet had a chance to arrange any meetings with her friends, their waiter, who had been eyeing them oddly ever since they had come into the restaurant, came over to their table.

"*Pardon, Monsieur,*" he said, bowing slightly. "But are you not Alain Gault?"

At the same time that Kristy started to say, "Why, yes, he is," she heard Alain saying, "No, I'm sorry, but you must have me confused with someone else."

"My mistake," the waiter said, looking confused. "Please excuse me."

As soon as he was out of earshot, Kristy looked over at Alain expectantly.

"Well? What was all that about?"

Alain seemed a bit disturbed by what had just happened. "Oh, nothing. It's just that . . . one of the odd things about this place is that when you make a reservation, sometimes the waiters take note of the name you've used and then they make a big deal about who you are."

"What?" Kristy wasn't following this at all. "I don't get it. You mean that the waiters here pretend you're somebody important just for the heck of it?"

"Something like that." Alain shrugged. "It's something that is very French. I don't think I could explain it very well."

Suddenly his face relaxed into a smile. "But I don't want to talk about the silly things that French people sometimes do. Today is your birthday, after all. We should be talking about you."

"What about me?" Kristy asked, suddenly nervous.

"Tell me more about your life at home, in the United States." With a teasing smile, Alain added, "I bet you are bothered by waiters and other people in restaurants all the time."

"Uh, yes, sometimes." Kristy shifted in her seat. "But, uh, mostly when I go out, I go to places where people won't recognize me or anyone in my family. I try to keep a low profile."

"A low profile?" Alain repeated. It was clear that this was one more English language expression that he didn't quite understand.

"You know, I make a real point of not acting like a celebrity. Mainly so I won't be recognized."

Just then, the waiter reappeared, this time carrying their appetizer. Kristy had suggested that Alain order for her, since he was so familiar with both the restaurant and, of course, the language. As she picked up a fork and dug into the mysterious-looking food that was artistically arranged on a small plate, she decided she would rather not know all the details of what she was eating.

Two hours later, after a magnificent meal that had been accompanied by equally memorable conversation, Kristy and Alain strolled through Paris. The night was lit up by stars and a bright, friendly moon. The breezes wafting off the Seine River were a refreshing change from the warm summer day. It couldn't have been more wonderful—at least, that was what Kristy was thinking *before* Alain reached over and gently took hold of her hand.

"You know, Kristy," he said in a soft voice, "sometimes I worry."

"Worry? About what, Alain?"

"I think you are very . . . very special. Sometimes, in fact, I cannot believe I have had the good luck to meet such a wonderful girl like you. And then I think about all the other boys you must know back at home, rich boys from important families, the kinds of boys who live the same kind of life as you."

Kristy was growing alarmed. "Oh, Alain, I don't care about that! Really! Most of the boys who are . . . who are like that are positively *boring*."

"Really? You find rich boys boring?"

"Well, sure. All they ever talk about is the new car they just bought or the expensive vacation they're about to go on or their new CD player. . . . Frankly, I find you a refreshing change."

"Do you really?" Alain let out a sigh of relief. "And here I thought that, sooner or later, you might begin to find that our differences were getting in our way."

"Oh, no, Alain. Not at all."

"Good. I'm so glad, Kristy."

They were standing on one of the gently arching stone bridges that stretched across the Seine, and suddenly Alain stopped walking. She could see that beyond the bridge, all of Paris stretched out before them, lit up by thousands of lights, looking like something out of a dream. And then Alain turned Kristy toward him and kissed her.

"So you think perhaps you could fall in love with a poor boy like me?" he asked in a soft voice.

Kristy, overwhelmed, simply nodded. She was too caught up in her own emotions to say what she was really thinking. And that was that she already had.

The light of the city so early in the morning, pale and uncertain as the sun cautiously made its way over the horizon, made the gray buildings of Paris look as if they were glowing. Nina sat at her bedroom window, her elbows resting on the sill, gazing out at the city spread out before her. Even now, after all these weeks, she was still overwhelmed by how breathtaking it all was: the graceful architecture, the narrow streets, the air of romance and beauty that lingered in the air day and night.

Oddly enough, she wasn't at all tired even though she had not slept a wink all night. She had lain in her bed in a tangle of sheets, staring at the clock, at first trying to sleep, but in the end resigning herself to a long night of doing nothing but waiting for morning to come.

Yet it was not the beauty of the city that had kept her up, or got her out of bed just as dawn was breaking.

It was thinking about Pierre.

Now that they had admitted that they were in love, everything had changed. He was more than just a summer romance, a little flirtation she was having while she was in Paris. This was something much more than puppy love. It was real, and it demanded that she make a choice.

She knew what that choice was. In fact, it was what she had been agonizing over for hours, staring at the flickering shadows on the ceiling as she tossed and turned in her bed. Finally she had gotten up, gone over to her dresser drawer and taken the stack of letters tied with a ribbon. Then she sat down in front of the window, the letters in her lap, and thought.

Having to make a decision about what to do was not made any easier by recognizing that she was in the exact same predicament her grandmother had been in fifty years earlier. Like her grandmother, Nina had come to Paris to learn and experience some of life, never expecting anything more complicated than problems with the language or having to learn a new system of money. Like her grandmother, she had been totally unprepared for the emotional tidal wave that took her captive after she met a very special young man.

And again, just like her grandmother, Nina now had to choose between staying with that young man and doing what was expected of her—what had always been expected of her—by her friends, her teachers . . . and especially her parents.

Her parents. She thought of them often, although not in the way she always had before. In the past, she had taken them for granted, seeing them as little besides her mother and her father. Now, suddenly, she saw them as two adults whose lives were the result of the decisions they had made. She realized that everyone, including them, constantly came to forks in the road, junctures at which they had to make choices. And very often, that choice was like the one she was now facing: a choice between what others wanted for her and what she knew in her heart was really right for her, even though it was bound to hurt those who loved her.

Her grandmother, Nina knew, had chosen the safer route, the one that was easier. True, it had caused her great emotional turmoil. It seemed, in fact, that she had never really gotten over the heartbreak of leaving behind the great love of her life. But at least she had escaped from having to take a real risk, of facing her family's disapproval . . . perhaps even their condemnation.

Nina sighed. The irony of having that same situation repeated all over again was not wasted on her. But it still didn't make her decision any easier—nor did it make it clearer to her which path she should follow.

She leafed through the letters, hoping that, somehow, touching them, feeling the paper beneath her fingers, would help her. She was frustrated when she realized that all she held in her hands was a piece of someone else's life.

"Grandmama," she suddenly cried aloud, "tell

me what I should do. Should I go back home and start college in the fall, the way Mom and Dad expect? Or should I throw all caution to the wind and follow my heart, staying on in Paris . . . staying with Pierre?"

But there was no answer forthcoming. All there was was a stack of letters, the silence of the early morning, and the knowledge that this was one decision that could be made by no one but her.

"What is the matter, *ma petite*?" Pierre asked, reaching over and stroking Nina's hair. "You are so quiet tonight."

He and Nina had just spent a long, busy day together, sight-seeing. It had been his idea that the two of them take in many of the city's attractions that tourists usually headed to the very first thing but which Nina had put off. Immediately after her morning classes, they had had a quick lunch, then dashed around the city, with Pierre in the lead, seeing as many spots as they could.

They had started at the famous cathedral of Notre-Dame, the breathtaking cathedral in the heart of the city that had taken almost two centuries to build. They laughed together over the famous gargoyles, the statues of grotesque demons along the top of the building. Nina even bought a gargoyle candlestick holder from one of the tourist shops nearby.

Their next stop was a church that was smaller and lesser known, but certainly no less beautiful. Sainte-Chapelle was once a palace chapel, best known for its stunning stained glass windows, the original ones that had been built in the late 1400s. Then they crossed over the Seine River on a bridge called the Pont au Change, heading toward the controversial Pompidou Center, *Le Centre Pompidou*. This unusual contemporary building housed a permanent modern art collection, as well as numerous art exhibits that bordered on the unusual. The area surrounding the Pompidou Center was filled with trendy boutiques, and as tired as they were, they dragged themselves through the narrow streets to window-shop.

It had been fun, but Pierre had sensed that, somehow, Nina's heart had not been in it. She was quiet and introspective, so much so that he had frequently stopped in mid-sentence as he was explaining some bit of history or telling an amusing anecdote about one of the sites they were visiting, saying, "Nina! Where are you, Nina? You are certainly not here with me."

Even now, at the top of the glorious Eiffel Tower, for most people the very symbol of Paris, she was having a difficult time keeping her mind on what she was doing. As they gazed across the beautiful city spread out before them, starting to quiet down as dusk crept slowly across the cloudless summer sky, she found that tears were forming in her eyes.

"Nina, I have tried not to put pressure on you," Pierre finally said, partly exasperated, partly sympathetic. "But all day you have been . . . in another world. There is something wrong, isn't there?"

"Not anything that hasn't been wrong all along," she answered enigmatically. She was staring off at the view, unable to meet his eyes.

Pierre, puzzled, cocked his head to one side.

Then he reached his finger under her chin and gently pulled her face up toward his.

"I do not understand," he said. "What is this . . . this thing that you claim has been wrong for such a long time?"

"Don't you know?" she cried. "Why, the fact that in less than three weeks, I'm supposed to get on that plane and leave. If everything goes according to plan, I'll just fly away, after saying good-bye to Paris . . . after saying good-bye to you."

With that, she burst into tears.

Pierre wrapped his arms around her and pulled her closer to him. She rested her head on his shoulder, meanwhile letting the tears fall, tears she had been holding back for so long that it actually felt good to get them out.

And then she heard his soft voice, right next to her ear. "You know, Nina, you don't have to leave."

Nina pulled away, her expression suddenly serious. "I-I know we talked about that before," she said haltingly, "but that was always just a fantasy . . . wasn't it?"

"For you, perhaps. But for me, it has always seemed like a very real possiblity."

"But my parents," she argued, her voice choking. "I don't want to hurt them."

"How would you be hurting them? I am afraid I truly do not understand."

"They expect certain things from me. They want certain things for me. They try to protect me."

A small grin crept over his face. "Forgive me for smiling, Nina. But I can't help wondering what it is your parents are so anxious to protect you from? Surely not from me, a poor but ambitious

French painter who is said to have at least a little bit of talent?"

Despite herself, Nina laughed. "My parents are just used to doing things the way they're supposed to be done. You grow up, you go to college, you establish a career for yourself—something practical like, like, oh, I don't know, accounting or teaching—and then you try to meet a nice man so you can get married and buy a house and then you have children and . . ."

Pierre burst out laughing. "You make it sound so dreadful! It doesn't have to be, you know."

"I know. And the truth is that it never seemed all that dreadful to me before. In fact, it all sounded kind of nice. Predictable and sensible and perfectly fine. But then. . . ."

"But then?" Pierre repeated.

"Then came you. And Paris. And the whole idea of having a different kind of life. One that isn't quite so . . . so predictable."

"Wait a minute," Pierre said teasingly, holding up his hands. "I don't think there's anything at all wrong with finding work that you enjoy, and finding a wonderful person to share your life with, and even having children one day. In fact, perhaps one day down the road you would find that I am too much of a stick in the mud for you."

He grew serious once again. "But, tell me, Nina. When you think of staying here in Paris, instead of going back home to your parents and your college and your nice, predictable life, what exactly do you think of? What do you see yourself doing?"

Nina didn't have to think twice. "Writing." She could feel herself blushing as she went on. "You know that the idea of writing is something very special to me, something so special, in fact, that I hardly dare tell anyone about it for fear they will laugh and . . . and try to talk me out of it."

"It is true that it is not as practical as accounting," Pierre said, only half-joking. "But if it is what you truly want to do, then *not* doing it will only leave you feeling dissatisfied."

Nina nodded. "You know, Pierre, I keep thinking about my grandmother—"

"Your grandmother. Again!" He pretended to be exasperated. "What is it about your grandmother this time?"

But he put his arm around her, adding, "I know what you are thinking, Nina. That right now you are agonizing over the very same decision your grandmother made so many years ago. And I know that all your life you probably thought that your grandmother made the wrong decision."

Nina bit her lip, then said, "My grandmother made the only decision she could. Things were different then. And . . . and she was a different person from me."

"Ah, yes. That is certainly true." Pierre took his arm away and leaned against the iron railing that ran around the ledge of the topmost level of the Eiffel Tower. His back was toward the city, and his blue eyes were fixed on Nina's.

"So what about you, Nina Shaw?" he said quietly. "What is your decision going to be? Are you going to do what your grandmother did? Or are you going to break with family tradition and do what you really, really want to do?"

Nina looked at him for a long time. There he was, Pierre du Lac, the young man she had always dreamed of meeting, the young man she had always known, somehow, that she would meet. And behind him was all of Paris, glistening like some wonderful jewel as the sun drifted behind it, holding the promise of a wonderful new beginning, a wonderful new life.

Could I ever leave all this? she wondered. Could I really get on that plane and go back to what I left behind, knowing that, once upon a time, I had a chance to make all my dreams come true?

It was at that moment, with Pierre standing before her and all of Paris stretched out right behind him, that Nina made her decision.

8

"ARE YOU *SURE* YOU WOULDN'T JUST rather go to a movie?" Jennifer asked.

She stopped her primping in the mirror over her dresser just long enough to give Michèle a hopeful look. But the Cartiers' pretty, lively granddaughter just laughed.

"Jennifer Johnson, sometimes you really surprise me," she said in her thickly accented English. "You act as if you are this cool, confident American teenager who is so sure of herself that practically everything is—how do you say it?—underneath her."

"I think you mean 'beneath her,'" Jennifer corrected her, not without great reluctance.

"Whatever. You act as if you don't care about anything. But here you are, on the verge of going out to a small party to meet some of my Parisian friends, and you are so nervous that you are trying to talk me out of taking you there!"

"Me? *Nervous?*" Jennifer whirled around. There was an angry scowl on her face.

But it wasn't long before she forced herself to laugh. It came out sounding weak and insincere, not at all the way she intended. "If you think I'm nervous about meeting a bunch of your friends, you're crazy. The only thing I'm afraid of is that I'll be bored to tears!"

Michèle's dark eyebrows shot up. "Oh, this is something you will not have to worry about. In fact, I can practically guarantee that the one thing you will not be tonight is bored."

Who cares about a bunch of French kids? Jennifer told herself as she and Michèle got off the métro on Paris's Left Bank, in a neighborhood not far from the Sorbonne. So what if I don't like them? And so what if they don't like me? she thought with much less enthusiasm.

Even so, the argument she was having with herself wasn't doing much to banish the butterflies from her stomach.

Jennifer was surprised when the door of the apartment was opened and she peeked inside. There were almost twenty young people packed into the living room, sitting on the couch or on the floor or standing around in groups of three or four. All of them were talking enthusiastically in French.

"Hello, everyone!" Michèle called gaily.

In response to her introduction, the party guests glanced up. All of them smiled in welcome. Almost immediately a boy and a girl about Jennifer's age came over, looking very pleased to see them.

"Ah, Michèle, I am so glad you could make it tonight!" A perky young woman with very short, very spiky dark hair leaned forward and kissed Michèle on each cheek. "And this must be your American friend."

"*Oui, c'est* Jennifer." Michèle placed a friendly hand on her shoulder. "Jennifer, this is Claudine.

Her English is only so-so, but I hope you will become friends anyway."

Claudine frowned. "You do not speak French?"

"Not everyone does, you know," Jennifer snapped.

"I think what Claudine means," the boy interrupted in a patient tone, speaking in excellent English, "is that one would expect someone like you who has chosen to come live in France for the summer to speak fairly good French."

"I see Michèle has already told you all about me," Jennifer returned coldly.

"Yes, she has," the boy replied with a friendly smile. "And we have been most eager to meet you. I myself spent the summer in the United States, three years ago. I have an uncle in Kentucky."

"Kentucky! That's nowhere near where I'm from. I'm from Connecticut."

"Well, then, I am even more anxious to hear all about Connecticut from a native like you." The boy, who had light brown hair and green eyes, held out his hand, as if to shake. "By the way, my name is Louis." With a laugh, he added, "When I was in Kentucky, everyone insisted on calling me 'Lou.' "

Reluctantly, Jennifer shook his hand. When he held on to it a second or two longer than was necessary, she was surprised to find that she didn't mind. As soon as she realized that, she withdrew it, sticking it in her pocket.

"Come and sit down." Already Claudine and Michèle had wandered off, and Jennifer was left alone with Louis. "How are you enjoying your stay in Paris so far?"

Having no choice, Jennifer followed him over to

the couch and sat down. "I guess it's okay. Michèle's been showing me around quite a bit. It's a good thing, too, since the people I'm staying with, her grandparents, are real duds."

"Duds?" Louis repeated, frowning.

"Oh, right. I keep forgetting that the people around here who say they can speak English are never really as up on the language as they claim. What I mean is, Madame and Monsieur Cartier are pretty dull."

"Dull?" This time, when Louis repeated what she had said, he sounded as if he couldn't quite believe he had heard her correctly.

But there was no time to explain. From the opposite corner of the room, what had been a quiet conversation suddenly exploded into a full-fledged argument.

"What do you mean? It is cause for emergency action!" one young woman was yelling in French.

"Yes, but it is the government's responsibility—" the boy she was talking to shot back.

"The government? The government?" the girl cried. "Since when has the government dealt satisfactorily with the concerns of the people?"

"What's going on?" Jennifer asked Louis, her voice a whisper. "My French isn't that great, although I think I caught most of what they're saying. What's so important that those two are fighting about it?"

"The environment," Louis replied calmly. "Monique feels that the pollution of the earth is such an extreme problem that it calls for emergency action, beginning with involvement from every single French citizen."

"It sounds like she wants a revolution," Jennifer commented, only half-joking.

Louis nodded seriously. "I think that is what she is saying."

Jennifer opened her mouth to reply. But before she could get any words out, Monique had crossed the room and was addressing her in rapid, loud French.

"What about the United States?" she demanded. "What are the private citizens over there doing to stop industry from ruining the air we breathe and the water we drink? What kind of stand is the most powerful nation in the world taking on this issue?"

Jennifer was too astonished to speak. She just stared at the girl standing with her face right in front of hers, yelling.

"Monique," Louis said, "Jennifer's French is probably not good enough for her to understand what you're saying."

"Ah, typical American!" Monique cried. "Why learn anything besides one's own language? Why look beyond one's own comfortable, convenient existence? Why concern oneself with anyone else's problems?" Haughtily she tossed her head. "Typical American attitudes!"

"Monique, I really think you're being too hard on Jennifer. She just got here. Why don't you fight your battles with someone who can at least understand what you're saying?"

Monique finally moved on, still arguing with the others, some of whom seemed to agree with her and some of whom seemed anxious to calm her down. Jennifer turned to Louis.

"I guess I should thank you for saving me."

Louis shrugged. "It did not seem like a fair fight. Monique is right, I believe, but she does tend to get carried away. Sometimes she attacks the wrong people."

"Like me," Jennifer agreed. "I mean, I'm not interested in getting all bent out of shape over pollution."

Louis seemed surprised. "But surely you are concerned?"

"Oh, I don't know. I guess I feel I'll just let other people worry about it."

"You don't think it is important for everyone to become involved in the issues that really matter?"

"I haven't really thought about it." Already Jennifer was growing bored. "Hey, this is supposed to be a party, isn't it? Isn't there anything to eat?"

Louis was still staring at her, as if he were puzzled. "There is some food in the kitchen. Come, I'll show you."

For the rest of the evening, he stuck by her, introducing her around, translating when she was having trouble understanding, smoothing over the difficulties of being the only stranger in the room. She found that she was feeling comfortable with him, even laughing at some of his jokes.

It was while she was laughing that he reached over and took her hand.

"I am glad to see you are having a good time," Louis said, his eyes shining with sincerity.

Jennifer stopped laughing. "Well, I wouldn't go that far," she said on impulse. Then, realizing how harsh her words sounded, she added, "But I do appreciate how kind you're being to me, Louis."

"Ah. Then perhaps you will be willing to see me

again. I would love to take you to some of my favorite parts of Paris."

Immediately Jennifer stiffened. 'Well, uh, thanks, but I kind of have a boyfriend already. You know, back at home. In Connecticut."

Louis looked amused as he said, "I am not asking to marry you, Jennifer. I simply asked if I could accompany you on some sight-seeing trips."

"Oh." Jennifer could feel herself turning pink. "Sure. I guess that would be okay."

Later, on the métro as the girls made their way back to the Cartiers', Michèle turned to Jennifer and said, "It looks as if you and Louis were really—how do you say—hitting it off."

Jennifer just shrugged. "Oh, he's okay, I guess. I think he felt sorry for me, being the only foreigner in the room and all."

Michèle laughed. "Louis? No, I don't think he felt sorry for you, Jennifer. I think he liked you." Glancing over at Jennifer with a twinkle in her eyes, she added, "Is that so terrible?"

"I already have a boyfriend," Jennifer returned. "I don't think he'd appreciate me running around Paris with some other guy."

"It is nice to see that you are committed to something," Michèle said under her breath, so softly that Jennifer wasn't sure she had heard her correctly.

In fact, she was about to ask Michèle to repeat what she had just said. In the end, however, Jennifer decided just to let it go.

"Don't worry, Kristy," Alain said anxiously. "I will not embarrass you today, I promise."

"Don't be silly," she replied. "Why on earth would you expect me to think you might do that?"

He shrugged. "It is just that I am nothing but a poor French boy and you . . . you . . . well, you know."

It would have been difficult to say which one of them was more nervous about the plans they had made for today. Kristy had finally agreed to allow Alain to get to know one of her American friends. While both of them had reservations about the afternoon, bringing him together with a friend from back home seemed impossible to put off any longer.

Kristy had chosen Jennifer, mainly because she and Alain already knew each other, at least a little bit. She was, of course, terrified that Jennifer would spill the beans about her true identity. She had thought of telling her about the little game she was playing with Alain, but every time an opportunity to do so came up, she found that she was tongue-tied.

So she simply hoped for the best as she and Alain made their way toward the sprawling and magnificent Louvre, the city's world-famous art museum. At least Jennifer would be pleased, she knew. She was always trying to get Kristy to spend more time with her, acting as if she and Nina were leaving her stranded by preferring to take advantage of the time they were living in a foreign country rather than spending the bulk of their time hanging around with other Americans.

Even so, she was well aware that Jennifer Johnson had never been known for her sensitivity—or her sense of diplomacy.

If we can only get through this afternoon with-

out Jennifer saying anything that will make Alain realize that I'm not who I say I am, Kristy thought with a loud sigh as she and Alain headed toward the front entrance of the impressive museum, I'll be a happy, happy girl.

The building that was now the Louvre had at one time been the largest palace in Europe. During the French Revolution, however, it was claimed by the people. The artwork that had formerly been privately owned by royalty was also put on display to be enjoyed by everyone.

Nowadays, the museum contained extensive collections of art that spanned the history of the world, beginning with Egyptian, Greek, and Roman antiquities, through medieval and Renaissance art, all the way up to artwork of the twentieth century. It was impossible to see it all; the wonders inside the museum were so plentiful that it would take a lifetime to do it all justice.

But Kristy was thinking about neither the fascinating history of this building nor the incredible collection of art inside as she caught sight of Jennifer. She was standing right inside the entrance at which they had planned to meet. She waved at Kristy and Alain as soon as they walked in.

"Kristy! Over here!" Jennifer called loudly, not taking the slightest notice of how many heads turned at the sound of her voice.

"So I finally get to check out this mystery man you've been keeping away from me as much as possible." Jennifer was looking Alain up and down. "I can't wait to see what the big deal is."

"Jennifer, Alain does speak English," Kristy reminded her, not even trying to keep the annoyance out of her voice.

"More or less, anyway, at least from what I've heard," Jennifer returned. She extended her hand toward Alain. "Well, Al, I'm glad I'll finally get the chance to get to know you a little," she said in that same loud voice. "Let's check out some of this art, okay?"

While Kristy was sensitive to every social blunder that her friend made, Alain seemed to like Jennifer very much. In fact, the two of them spent most of the time talking together, leaving Kristy pretty much on her own. What bothered her most about that arrangement was that she couldn't hear what Jennifer was saying—and she couldn't always see Alain's reaction, either. She only hoped that they were talking about the collection of Egyptian mummies they were poring over.

And as far as she could tell, that did seem to be the case. That is, until the three of them sat down on a bench, tired after spending more than an hour thoroughly covering the museum's entire section on Ancient Egypt.

"Wow, this is some big place," Jennifer commented, fanning herself with the map she had been carrying around, rolled up in her hand.

"You must have big museums near your home," Alain said. "You live very close to New York City, don't you?"

"Oh, sure," Jennifer returned. "But we hardly ever go in. At least, not to the museums. Oh, sure, we go in for shopping, and sometimes to the movies—"

"Ah, yes. The movies. Do you ever see Kristy or her mother in the movies?"

Jennifer looked puzzled for a moment, then remembered that Alain's English was not all that strong. "Oh sure, sometimes. Especially when we were younger. Then, Kristy's mom was usually the one who drove us to the movies or the malls or whatever. But my friends and I pretty much go on our own these days."

Kristy, meanwhile, was holding her breath. But before Alain had a chance to try to clarify this point any further, however, she interrupted.

"Hey, I'm getting kind of hungry," she said. "Anybody else here want to find the restaurant? I would love a Coke or something cold."

"Not me," Jennifer said. "To be perfectly honest, I can't believe the cost of most things in this town."

"Ah, so your family is not like Kristy's, then?" Alain asked innocently.

Jennifer cast him an odd look as Kristy answered the question for her.

"What he means, Jen, is that, uh, my parents sent me off on this trip with all the spending money I could possibly need. I haven't had to worry about things like the cost of Cokes."

Alain laughed, thinking she was making a real understatement. Jennifer, meanwhile, was looking at them both strangely.

Kristy was wondering how much more of this she was going to be able to take when Alain said, "Well, Jennifer, it must be nice to go sight-seeing with Kristy in a place like Paris, where no one is likely to recognize her."

"Huh?" By this point, Jennifer was totally lost. "What are you two talking about?"

But Alain just shrugged. "Jennifer, I am so sorry that my English is not very good. Don't worry. I am very used to having people who speak English not understand what I am saying." He smiled fondly at Kristy. "That is, unless they are willing to be patient and listen to me with great care. But that is the rare person indeed."

"Listen, I'm suddenly feeling lots perkier," Kristy said, jumping off the bench. "I don't want a Coke, after all. Let's go find the Ancient Greek stuff. I understand there's a really terrific exhibit of marble statues somewhere around here."

So far, I've managed to get through this afternoon without anything deadly happening, Kristy was thinking, wiping her damp palms on her skirt. But I'd be better off keeping them both distracted. If they're talking about Greek statues, they're less likely to start talking about anything that'll blow my cover.

But the pressure is really getting to me. After today, I think I'm going to have to continue to keep Alain away from the people who know the "real" Kristy Connor.

Either that, she knew, or tell him the truth. And after the night of her birthday dinner, when she had realized she was in love with him and he had told her his true feelings for her—or at least for the Kristy he *thought* she was—she was in no hurry to take a risk like that. Not now, when all of a sudden, the stakes were a lot higher than they had ever been before.

"Hello, Mom? Is that you? Yes, it's really me! It's Nina!"

She hoped the nervousness that insisted upon creeping into her voice wasn't too obvious. And Nina was nervous. After all, she wasn't just calling her parents, three thousand miles away, to assure them she was in good health and having a good time. No, this was about something much more important.

She had thought of writing it down in a letter but had realized quickly that that simply would not do. It was true that up until this point, she had written her parents wonderful letters, at least once a week. They were long ones, four or five pages at a time, filled with detailed descriptions of the places she had visited, the courses she was taking, the people she had met. Pierre du Lac had been mentioned in those letters, but only in passing.

But now it was time for her to speak to them in person. Not only about Pierre but also about the decision she had come to.

"You sound so close," her mother said. "I can't believe how clearly your voice is coming across!" Nervously she added, "But really, Nina. This must be costing a fortune."

"It's not that expensive," Nina assured her, keeping the annoyance out of her voice. "Besides, there's something special I have to tell you. Somehow, a letter just didn't seem good enough."

"Oh, dear. There's something wrong, isn't there?" her mother breathed. "Nina, honey, are you all right?"

"What's the matter? What happened?" Her father's voice suddenly came booming over the wires as, back in Connecticut, he picked up the extension. "Nina, why are you calling? What's wrong?"

"Nothing is wrong, Dad. Everything is fine. Really." Nina took a deep breath. This was going to be even harder than she had anticipated.

Suddenly needing a little moral support, she

glanced over at Pierre, sitting in the corner of the Rousseaus' apartment. He mouthed the words, ''I love you.'' Instead of making her feel better, however, it just made her stomach tighten up a little bit more.

''Isn't this awfully expensive?'' her father was saying. ''What does a transatlantic call go for these days?''

''I'm not sure,'' Nina said, sounding much more patient than she was feeling. ''I don't intend to talk for a long time. But there is something special I want to talk to you about.''

At the other end of the telephone wires, her parents were silent. Nina gripped the telephone receiver so tightly that her knuckles were white.

''Mom, Dad, I-I've reached kind of a decision. I'm, uh, hoping you'll support me in it, because I've given it a lot of thought . . . and I know that it's what's really best for me.''

''Go on,'' her mother said in a pinched voice.

''I've decided that when the summer is over, I'm . . . uh, I'm . . .'' Nina took a deep breath and then let out a sigh. ''I'm going to stay here in Paris.''

''*What?*'' her father cried. ''You're going to do *what?*''

''I'm going to stay—''

''Nina, have you completely lost your senses?'' Mr. Shaw barked. ''What on earth are you talking about? What about college? Just yesterday in the mail you got your class schedule. You were even accepted into that creative writing class you wanted to take.''

''That's . . . that's great, Dad. And, in fact, writing happens to be one of the reasons I've decided to stay here. I thought being on my own in Paris would give me a good chance to try doing some serious writing. Of course, I'll get a job, too, something to support me—"

"I think I understand what's going on here," her mother interrupted. "You've met a boy, haven't you, Nina?"

"Have you, Nina?" her father echoed.

"Why, yes, as a matter of fact. I wrote you about him. His name is Pierre du Lac, and you'll never believe—"

"Now that's just great," Mr. Shaw said. "You're going to throw away your college education, your whole future, for some . . . some French boy you've got a silly crush on."

"It's not like that!" Nina found herself doing precisely what she had promised herself she wouldn't do: exploding. "You just don't understand! Pierre and I love each other! And that's only part of it. Don't you see? I want to live here! I love it in Paris. I belong here. It's . . . it's not like Connecticut, and it's not some boring, sleepy little town. And the Sorbonne is filled with exciting people who are really interested in doing something with their lives."

"Nina, this is utterly ridiculous," Mr. Shaw said. "You're talking like a child. I thought you knew better than to lose your head over some stupid boy. Now listen to me. You're coming back with the other students from your school, just as we've planned all along, and that's final."

There were tears in Nina's eyes, but her voice sounded controlled as she said, "No, Daddy. This is one time when I know what I really want. I know I've never gone against your wishes before, not even for the smallest thing. I took the courses you wanted me to take in school; I applied to the college you wanted me to go to. . . . I even decorated my bedroom to suit you and wore clothes that you approved of.

"But I'm not a little girl anymore. This time I've made up my mind. I'm going to stay in Paris."

"I have the best news, Pierre!" Nina announced in her flawless French.

It was two days after her triumphant telephone call to her parents—her "declaration of independence," as she now thought of it. Since then, she had been walking on air. But she had been doing even more than that: she had been making plans.

Now, as she threw open the door of the art studio, almost bursting with her good news, she found Pierre exactly as she had expected to find him: standing at his easel, paintbrush in hand, taking advantage of the last rays of the late afternoon sun. Set up in front of him on a wooden straight-back chair was a vase of wildflowers, vibrant shades of purple and blue and yellow. Directly behind it was the backdrop he had made by draping blue fabric across the back of the chair.

Nina glanced over at the setup, noting that the arrangement of flowers was actually rather ordinary. On Pierre's canvas, however, it looked magnificent.

But she was not here to be an art critic.

"It's really wonderful news," she went on, crossing the room. "See if you can guess."

"I know," he said, depositing his brush in a glass jar of turpentine. "You had lunch today with a publisher who is begging you to let him publish your first novel—whenever it is finished."

Nina giggled and threw her arms around Pierre. "No, that hasn't happened yet."

"Not yet, but someday." Pierre frowned. "Let me see . . . I know! You stayed up all night and wrote the first chapter of your book."

"Pierre, maybe I'd better just come right out and tell you," Nina said with a sigh. "Otherwise, this could take all day."

"Believe me, there is no other way I would prefer to spend a day, other than talking to you. Unless, of course," Pierre added with a sly grin, "I could spend the whole day kissing you."

"Not now, my sweet." Gently she pushed him away, then pranced around the room in front of him. "Guess again!"

"I've got it! You have decided to become a ballerina."

"No." She stopped dancing and folded her arms across her chest. "Pierre," she said, her face flushed, "I found myself a place to live!"

In response to his puzzled expression, she went on, "You see, I can only stay with the Rousseaus until the end of the month. That was the original plan, after all. Anyway, when I decided to stay in Paris after the summer is over, I knew I had to find an apartment. I mentioned it to the Rousseaus, and it turned out that Madame Rousseau has a sister with a town house not too far from here.

"And," she continued gleefully, clapping her hands, "Madame's sister will be thrilled to rent me the top floor! I haven't seen it yet, but she says there's a bathroom up there, and while I won't have my own kitchen, I can use the woman's any time I want. She's hardly ever around, since she works for Air France and is always traveling . . . So?" Nina threw her arms out, as if she were asking a question. "What do you think?"

He stared back at her, blinking. "It sounds too wonderful to be true. When do I get to see it?"

With a twinkle in her dark brown eyes, Nina reached into the pocket of her jeans and pulled out a shiny gold key. "Is the prospect of seeing my first apartment enough to drag you away from your painting?"

"Nina," he replied, coming over to her and taking her arm, "have I ever been able to say no to you?"

The apartment on the top floor of Madame Rousseau's sister's house was even better than what Nina had been expecting. It consisted of two good-sized rooms plus a bathroom, all on the third floor of a narrow brick house no more than half a mile away from Pierre's art studio. The rooms were bright and airy with large windows and pale green walls. There were even a few pieces of furniture: a sagging couch and a table in the front room, a bed and a large wooden dresser in the other.

To some people, it probably wouldn't have looked like much. But to Nina, it was heaven on earth.

"Pierre, this is fantastic!" she cried, walking back and forth between the two rooms, still barely able to believe her good luck. "I'll make this room a combination living room and study. I'll get a big wooden desk for that corner over there, so I can work in front of that big window. I'll get something serious-looking, the kind of thing a writer would use. And I'll make this smaller room in the back the bedroom. I'll make it come alive with pastels. I'll fill it with wonderful fabrics and rag rugs and vases of fresh flowers. . . ."

"Don't forget the paintings," Pierre said.

"The paintings? What paintings?"

"Why, my paintings, of course. The ones I'm going to create for you. If you'd like, you can line your walls with them."

He was only half-teasing as he added, "Of course, I do have an ulterior motive."

"You do?" Nina blinked. "What's that?"

"I want you to think about me all the time."

Nina's confused expression melted into a smile.

"Ah, Pierre," she said, throwing her arms around his neck, "I don't think you have to worry about that."

As they strolled back to the Rousseaus' to return the key Madame had lent her, Nina grew more pensive.

"Now almost everything is in place," she said, jamming her hands deep inside the pockets of her jeans.

"Almost?" Pierre seemed surprised. "And here I was just thinking about how impressed I was that you'd already taken care of every detail."

"*Almost* every detail." Nina frowned. "I still need a job. I know finding one won't be easy, since it's not that simple for a foreigner like me, someone without French citizenship, to get working papers."

"Hmmm." Pierre was pensive. "How much money do you think you'll need to make?"

"I think I'll be able to live on very little. The rent that Madame's sister is charging me is such a small amount. I think that more than anything, she's just happy to have someone staying in her house since she's away so much. And my expenses will be low. I can eat cheaply, and it's not as if I have expensive art supplies to buy, the way you do. I'll have to get myself a typewriter, of course. . . ." She glanced over at Pierre. "Any ideas about what kind of job I could get?"

Pierre shook his head. "I am afraid not. But don't lose heart. You still have some time left before the summer ends."

Nina didn't reply. She was too busy thinking, Yes, there's still *some* time . . . but not very much.

And she knew perfectly well that without a job—some kind of job, any kind of job—her dream of staying here, of living in Paris, would simply fade away, gone before it had ever become a reality.

9

"KRISTY! WAIT UNTIL YOU HEAR WHAT HAS happened!"

There was a jubilant expression on Alain's face when Kristy came out of her last class of the morning and found him out in the hall, waiting for her. His green eyes were shining, and the smile on his face was so big and bright that it made his entire face light up.

"What is it? Alain, what happened?" His excitement, she was finding, was contagious.

"Oh, Kristy. I do not know where to begin."

"Can't you just come right out and tell me?"

Alain's smile faded into a frown. "Well . . . I would like to, but it is not quite that simple."

"What are you talking about, Alain? *What* is not so simple? Now I'm really confused."

He hesitated for a moment before saying, "Kristy, I think you had better sit down. Come, let us go get some lunch. I will tell you then."

The ten minutes between the time Alain announced that he had some important news to tell her and the time that the two of them were finally sitting on a bench in a small park near the Sorbonne, holding croissants filled with ham and cheese, seemed endless to Kristy. She had no idea what Alain had to tell her, but she had the sneaking suspicion that what was good news for him might well turn out to be not such good news for her.

"We're sitting down now," she said impatiently, ignoring her sandwich. "Now tell me, before I scream."

"All right. But I have to go back a little bit. Kristy, I told you back when you and I first met that I was interested in geology. And I believe I mentioned that my parents have never exactly been supportive of the idea of me following a career studying rocks." He made a face as he said, "They have always had more . . . shall we say, predictable plans for me."

Kristy wasn't sure she understood, but she nodded anyway. "Go on."

"Anyway, I secretly applied to a special program at a college with a very strong geology department, without telling them that no matter what they thought, I was still very serious about getting a Ph.D. in this field. They found out my little secret by accident, when the school wrote to me to ask for more information about my studies." With a frown, he explained, "They happened to see the envelope before I had a chance to hide it from them."

This was becoming more and more mysterious to Kristy. Why on earth would Alain's parents be against his studying geology . . . and getting a Ph.D. in such a respectable field, no less?

While she was trying not to prolong the introduction to his "good news" any more than necessary, she couldn't resist asking, "Alain, why are they so against this? It sounds wonderful to me."

He looked at her sadly. "Because they want me to take over the family business."

"Oh." Finally it was beginning to make some sense. "You mean their little store on the outskirts of Paris."

Alain nodded.

"But here you have an interest in doing something so much more important than simply running a tiny shop! You want to go on to get a good education for yourself, probably to be more successful than anyone else in your family has ever been. Why aren't they glad about that?"

"Because running the store is a family tradition. My grandfather started the business, and my father took it over after he finished his schooling. My parents always just assumed that when I finished at the Sorbonne—when I got bored with playing with my rocks and stones, was the way they put it—I, too, would be ready to learn the family business so I could continue to run it."

Kristy shrugged. "I guess people just feel differently here than they do in America. Most people would be thrilled if their kids wanted to get a Ph.D. Anyway, go on, Alain. You still haven't told me what your good news is."

"A few months ago, when my parents saw the envelope from the school I had applied to, we all sat down and had a long talk about my future. I tried very hard to make them understand about the things that are important to me. When I managed to make them see how much it means to me, they finally agreed that if—*if*—I got into this special program, they would send me off with their blessing. No more talk about the store. But if I wasn't accepted into the program—"

"But I bet you were, right?"

Alain nodded, his face relaxing into a huge grin.

"Oh, Alain! I'm so thrilled for you!" Kristy threw her arms around him. "I'm so glad you're going to get to do what you really want."

"Yes, but that's not even the very best part," Alain said, drawing away from her so he could see her face. "Kristy, I can hardly wait to tell you the rest of this."

"Then don't wait," Kristy said, laughing. "What is it, Alain?"

He took a deep breath before speaking. He was still wearing his huge smile as he said, "The school I'm going to is in Boston, Massachusetts. The same city where you are going to college in the fall!"

Suddenly the true meaning of his words dawned on her. Alain was coming to the United States to study. That was wonderful for him, but it meant that he was going to find out that she was a fraud!

Her spirits instantly sank. It was suddenly clear to her that what had begun as a kind of prank, an experiment to see what life would be like if she truly were the person she had always dreamed of being, had seriously backfired. As soon as Alain found out how sneaky she had been, he would want nothing to do with her. He would see her for what she really was . . . not only someone capable of tricking him for weeks on end, but also someone who, in reality, was a social zero, an absolute nothing. Whatever friendship existed between her and Alain, whatever romance was beginning to blossom . . . it would all be crushed when he found out that she was a phony.

Kristy felt like crying. But she knew that, for now at least, she had to pretend that everything was fine, that her happiness for him over being accepted into the academic program that was so important to him was untainted.

"Oh, Alain, that's so great," she cooed. "Really. I couldn't be happier for you."

"Not only for me, also for us!" he proclaimed triumphantly. "Kristy, this means we can still be together in the fall! We will be living in the same city. We don't have to go off on our separate ways just because the summer is over. Everything is working out perfectly."

Kristy forced a smile. "Everything is perfect," she said. "Completely, utterly perfect."

But she could already see the writing on the wall.

"Here, let me take your picture," Alain was saying, reaching for her camera. "I want to remember exactly how you look today. The day you found out that you and I were going to be together! I want to record this day, a day that for both of us is the best day of our lives!"

"Sure, Alain. Go ahead."

Halfheartedly Kristy struck a pose, hoping the two-dimensional, black-and-white image wouldn't expose the truth—that instead of its being the best day of her life, this was one of the worst.

"How about waitressing?" Kristy suggested, her tone of voice making it clear that she was trying to be helpful.

She was sitting cross-legged on the floor of the sunny front room on the third floor of Madame Rousseau's sister's house, the room that Nina was planning to turn into a living room and study when she moved in at the end of the summer. Immediately after their morning classes that day, Nina had insisted on bringing her two best friends over for a look at the dream apartment that, hopefully, would soon be hers.

"If you worked as a waitress, you could make a lot of money from tips," Kristy went on enthusiastically. "Hey, I know. Since you speak English, maybe you could work in a restaurant that specializes in tourists."

Nina, sitting on the floor beside her, made a face. "I don't want to live in Paris so that I can work around other Americans! Besides, restaurants are run differently here, remember? We learned that in our class on French culture. Waiters and waitresses don't get tipped in cash, the way they do at home. In France, a fifteen-percent service charge is automatically added on to every bill."

"Why anybody would want to stay here at *all* is beyond me," Jennifer grumbled, lounging on the threadbare couch. The oversized piece of furniture looked rather lonely, parked the way it was in the middle of the room. "I mean, this apartment is nice and everything, but I'm already counting the days until I can go home."

"Jen, you've been doing that since the moment we stepped off the plane," Kristy shot back.

Nina, meanwhile, chose to ignore Jennifer.

"Even waitressing would require working papers," she said, staring out the window at the charming town houses lined up below. There was also a small grocery across the street, an *épicier*. Already she was longing to make stopping in there for cheese and fruit and French bread a part of her everyday routine. In fact, just thinking about it made her heart ache with longing for the romantic, totally free existence that she imagined living in Paris would provide for her.

She let out a long, loud sigh. "I don't know how I'm ever going to get a job."

"If you need these . . . these working papers," Kristy said, "then why don't you just go get them?"

"It's not that simple," Nina replied. "Getting them requires applications, proof of residence, special documents . . . all kinds of maddening paperwork. Mostly, it requires time.

"And time happens to be the one thing I haven't got. We have less than two weeks left before we're scheduled to go home. If I don't have a job by then . . ."

"Well, look on the bright side," Kristy insisted. "You've already got yourself a great apartment. You've got good friends here, like Pierre and the Rousseaus. You even stood up to your parents and told them that, whether they liked it or not, you were going to stay. And they seem to have accepted it.

"Face it, you've been pretty lucky so far. And there's no reason in the world why your luck shouldn't hold up."

Nina just nodded. She had to believe that Kristy was right. To believe she *wasn't* right, after all, would have been just too depressing.

"How about you, Kristy?" she asked. "Are you like Jennifer here, already starting to think about going back home?"

"Well. . . ." Kristy swallowed hard. She was thinking about Alain—and the news he had delivered to her just the day before. "I guess I have started thinking about what it's going to be like going to school in Boston in the fall."

She was debating whether or not to say anything to her friends about the latest development with Alain when Jennifer cut in.

"What about Alain?" Mindlessly she pulled a loose thread out of the couch's slipcover fabric. "Aren't you two, like, madly in love or something? Aren't you going to miss him?"

"Yes, what about Alain?" Nina asked.

"As a matter of fact," Kristy said slowly, "he got some rather interesting news just the other day. He's, uh, going to school in Boston in the fall."

Nina jerked her head up. "Boston? You mean Boston, Massachusetts? The same Boston where you're going to college in September?"

Kristy just nodded.

"That's fantastic!" Nina cried. "Kristy, you must be in seventh heaven! I mean, it's been obvious from the start that you really like Alain. And he's made it clear that he's crazy about you. And now he's going to go back to the States the same time as you . . . things couldn't be better!"

"I guess so."

Nina frowned. "You don't seem very enthusiastic. Is there something wrong?"

Here it is, Kristy was thinking, another chance to tell them, another chance to get their advice. But the more her little white lie snowballed, the less likely it seemed that she would ever be able to tell anyone about it, no matter how much she wanted to.

So she just shrugged and said, "I guess I'm just surprised by the whole thing, that's all. I never expected in a million years that my relationship with Alain would continue past the summer."

"You don't have to continue it, you know," Nina said gently. "If you're not sure about him, that is."

"It's not that I don't like him. It's just that . . . well, I'll just have to wait and see what happens."

Anxious to change the topic of conversation before she said any more, Kristy said, "How about you, Jennifer? How has Danny been doing without you all summer? Has he been writing you letters?"

"Almost every day," Jennifer replied proudly. "And I've been writing to him every day, too. I've been telling him everything that's been happening to me."

"You must be writing very short letters," Kristy couldn't help commenting.

"And what's that supposed to mean?" Jennifer shot back.

"Nothing. Just that . . . well, you haven't exactly been going out of your way to make the most of your time in Paris. Even you have to admit that, Jen."

"I've been doing some interesting things," Jennifer sniffed, not wanting to be left out. "Just the other night, the Cartiers' granddaughter, Michèle, took me to a party so I could meet some of her friends."

"That was considerate of her," Nina said. "What were they like?"

Jennifer thought for a few seconds. "Some of them were really creepy. There was this one girl, Monique or something, who was all over me, criticizing Americans. I didn't like her at all."

"Weren't any of them nice?" Kristy asked, exasperated.

"Well . . . there was this one boy—"

"A boy?" Kristy and Nina cried in unison, instantly sitting up straighter. The two of them looked at each other and then burst out laughing.

"Okay," said Kristy. "Come on, spill the beans, Jen. Tell us all about him."

"To be perfectly honest, I'm not even sure I liked him all that much," Jennifer said slowly. "It's just that at this party, he was so darned *nice* to me."

"What's this?" Kristy said teasingly. "Jennifer Johnson met a French person who was actually *nice*? I think I'm going to faint!"

"Well, maybe they're not all bad," Jennifer admitted with great reluctance.

"So are you going to go out with this boy?" Nina asked eagerly.

"Oh, I don't think so," Jennifer said. "Louis— that's his name—Louis didn't even ask me for my telephone number. Besides, it's just as well."

Kristy looked at Nina, rolling her eyes upward. "Why is that, Jennifer? What's your excuse this time?"

"I'm just busy, that's all. Don't forget, we just got assigned those stupid oral reports on French history that we have to give the last week of classes."

"I'm looking forward to doing mine," Nina said. "I was lucky. The topic I was assigned is really interesting. I'm supposed to give a report on France right after the French Revolution."

"That's funny," Kristy said. "My topic is France right *before* the French Revolution. How about you, Jen? What's your topic?"

Jennifer made a face. "France during World War

II. What could possibly be more boring than that? Even so, I want to do a decent job on it. I mean, we do have to stand up in front of the entire class and give a twenty-minute report. I don't want to make a total fool of myself."

For a long time, the girls lapsed into silence. Each one was thinking about her own problems. For Jennifer, it was researching and writing a report that she was anything but enthusiastic about. For Kristy, it was worrying about how she would ever manage to maintain her false identity once Alain was on her home turf. For Nina, it was finding a job so that her dream of living in Paris could really come true. What was supposed to be a special, carefree time for each of the three girls was, at least at the moment, looking very, very complicated.

"Nina, I've had a brainstorm," Pierre said, appearing on the Rousseaus' doorstep late one afternoon. He was so excited about his *"idée de génie"* that he didn't even notice the distraught expression on Nina's face as she answered the door.

"A brainstorm?" Nina repeated. "Wait, Pierre, before you say anything, there's something important I have to tell you."

"It's a wonderful idea." Pierre came storming into the apartment, acting as if he hadn't heard a word she had said. "It's about your job." He plopped down in a big, overstuffed chair.

"What about my job? What's your brainstorm?" Despite herself, Nina was finding that Pierre's excitement was contagious.

"You don't have any working papers, right?"

"Right. . . ."

"And that means that you don't qualify for a regular job."

"Right."

"Well, then, I think I have found a solution. How about working for an individual, somebody who pays you out of his own pocket?"

"You mean doing something like baby-sitting?"

"That's one possibility. I was thinking more along the lines of being someone's personal assistant. Someone like—oh, I don't know, someone like an entrepreneur, someone who is in business for himself . . . or someone who works free-lance, maybe in a creative field. A writer, perhaps."

Nina was silent for a long time as she pondered Pierre's idea.

"That would be kind of exciting," she finally said, speaking slowly. "And it could turn out to be a good opportunity for me to learn. If I hooked up with the right person, that is."

"That," Pierre said, his wide grin suddenly fading, "is the only negative part of my idea."

"What is?"

He shrugged his shoulders, meanwhile looking at her in defeat. "Finding the right person."

Nina sighed. "Speaking about negatives," she said slowly, "I think you'd better give me a chance to tell you my news."

Pierre's expression darkened. "What has happened, Nina?"

"Well, maybe it's not *that* bad. I mean, it all depends on how you look at it. . . ."

She sank onto the couch, opposite Pierre.

"I just got a telephone call from my parents." There was something he had never seen before in her dark brown eyes, something that looked very much like fear. "Pierre, they're coming. They're coming to Paris." Her voice was hoarse, her words barely audible.

Pierre, meanwhile, was confused. "Your parents? They are coming here? But why?"

"To try to talk me out of staying on after the summer is over, that's why!"

"But . . . but I thought they had accepted what you told them. I thought they agreed that you were old enough to start making your own choices."

"That's what I thought, too." Nina sighed. "But it turns out they think I'm making a rash decision. At least, that's what they said on the phone just now. They finally came out and said all the things that I was so surprised they didn't say when I first told them about my plans. They think I'm doing a terrible thing, throwing away my future because of some ridiculous case of puppy love. . . ."

The tears that had been gathering in her eyes began sliding down her cheeks. "Oh, Pierre! They don't understand at all."

He got up and went over to the couch. Putting a protective arm around her, he said, "Nina, this is not such an awful thing. They simply want what is best for their daughter. They love you, and they want to keep you safe."

"They want to keep me a little girl."

"They want you to be happy. Who could blame them for that?" He lifted her wet face up to his. "What are you so afraid of, *ma chouchou*? That they will disapprove? You already know that they are not happy about your decision to stay here in Paris. And they are certainly not happy about the fact that you are starting to do what you think is best, instead of what they think is best for you.

Perhaps it will be a difficult visit. That, I can understand. But I will stay with you the whole time they are here, if it will make it easier for you."

She shook her head. "Thank you, Pierre. But this is something I must do alone. . . . Now, let's not let this ruin our afternoon together. I'm glad you came by, and I'd rather talk about happier things. Let's put our heads together and see if we can come up with any ideas of someone who might want to hire me as an assistant."

Nina took a deep breath, determined not to be too consumed by her nervousness about her parents' upcoming visit. She knew their purpose was to talk her out of staying on in Paris, pursuing her dream of writing, remaining with the young man she loved. While she recognized that they were only doing what they thought was best, and that they were doing it out of love for her, she was still resentful.

Don't they trust me? she thought. Don't they realize that I am old enough, and capable enough, to start making my own decisions? Can't they accept that only I know what's best for me? Don't they understand what it means to have a dream?

Even more than feeling resentful, she realized, she was feeling afraid. After all, there was one possibility that was too frightening to tell Pierre about, or even to admit fully to herself. And that was the possibility that her mother and father would actually succeed in their mission of talking her out of her decision to stay in Paris.

10

"MOM! DAD! WELCOME TO PARIS!"

Nina hoped that her greeting sounded sincere as she stood at Gate 14 of Charles de Gaulle Airport, waving wildly at her parents as they filed off the plane and into the lounge. She was truly happy to see them, not having realized up until this moment just how much she had missed them. Even so, the butterflies in her stomach would not let her forget that her mother and father were here to do a lot more than visit the Eiffel Tower and the other sights of Paris.

"So this is Paris," Mr. Shaw grumbled. He hoisted his heavy tote bag over his shoulder, looking around the airport with a frown. "If you ask me, it looks like it's as bad as New York."

"How was your flight?" Nina asked cheerfully. "Here, Mom, let me carry that for you."

"The flight was all right, I guess." Mrs. Shaw sounded tired as she handed her overnight bag to her daughter. "It was just so . . . so *long*."

"Look at this. All the signs are in French," Mr. Shaw observed. He sounded as if he were taking it personally. "How on earth am I supposed to understand anything while I'm here?"

"I'll translate for you, Dad," Nina said. "Well,

at least you both got here in one piece. Do you have any other luggage?''

"Tons of it," Mr. Shaw said. "Your mother brought half the house with her. She even brought toilet paper."

"Toilet paper?" Nina stopped in her tracks. "Mom, they have toilet paper here."

"Well, now, I wasn't sure it would be the kind I'm used to. You know me. I'm the kind of person who likes things to be predictable."

"That's right," Mr. Shaw agreed heartily, sounding proud of his wife. "No surprises for this lady."

"Nina, I'm a total wreck," Mrs. Shaw said. "I don't suppose there's anywhere I'll be able to take a hot shower, is there?"

"Mother, you'll find that Paris is a very civilized place," Nina said in an even voice. "Not only do we have toilet paper, we even have hot water."

Her father cast her an odd look at her use of the word "we." She simply ignored it, instead attempting to change the subject.

"I hope you're planning on staying long enough to see some of the sights. There are so many wonderful museums and cathedrals, and of course the *châteaux*, the castles, if you're up for a trip out of the city. . . ."

"We plan to stay only as long as it takes to talk you out of this cockamamy idea of yours," Mr. Shaw said. He was talking so loudly that several people turned around to look at him. "Unless, of course, you've already come to your senses."

Nina's silence told them she had not changed her mind about her decision to stay. Her mother quickly tried a new tack.

"You know, Nina," she said pleasantly as she followed her daughter through the crowded airport, toward the exit, "your father came up with the most wonderful idea. Instead of all three of us leaving together from Paris, he thought that once you got all your things packed up, we could take a week or two and see some of Europe. You know, travel—all three of us, as a family—to Holland, Spain, Germany . . . wherever you like."

The true meaning of her words was not wasted on Nina. Her mother was offering her a bribe. Come home with us, she was saying, be a practical, obedient daughter who does what we think is best for her, and we'll reward you with a trip around Europe.

Instead of feeling at all enticed, however, or even the least bit sympathetic to what they were feeling, Nina was simply irritated. "Perhaps you two would enjoy traveling around a bit," she said. "It would give you a chance to have kind of a second honeymoon." She couldn't resist adding, "Surely you don't want a third wheel getting in your way, spoiling your time alone together."

Mrs. Shaw, seeing she wasn't going to get anywhere, quickly dropped it. "Nina, I'm exhausted," she said as the threesome piled into a taxi. "Your father and I both need to get some rest. That plane ride was endless. Half the time your dad was as white as a ghost."

"I was fine," Mr. Shaw insisted. "I just had a little indigestion, that's all. That food they serve on airplanes leaves a lot to be desired."

"At any rate, I'm not going to be any good to anybody until I have had a shower, a nap, and a good hot meal. I'm desperate for a cup of tea."

Mrs. Shaw peered at her daughter. "Nina, honey, it *is* safe to drink the water here, isn't it?"

It wasn't until that evening that Mr. and Mrs. Shaw pronounced themselves ready to reenter the world again. Just as they had promised, they had spent their first day in Paris resting at the hotel. Nina, meanwhile, took advantage of her unexpected free time to seek out Pierre.

"So how do your parents like Paris so far?" he asked. They were strolling along the Seine together, watching the *bateaux mouches*, the tour boats, sailing along lazily. The tiny dots that were the people riding on them, Parisians and tourists alike, were glued to the sides, ogling the unparalleled view of the city that traveling down the city's main waterway afforded them.

"So far, they've done nothing but complain," Nina returned. "Honestly, you'd think they were visiting Mars or something."

"Nina, to them Paris might as well be Mars," Pierre reminded her, amused.

"Well, I'm just warning you. Don't be insulted if it turns out they're not the least bit interested in meeting my favorite Martian," Nina said with a scowl.

Her prediction turned out to be wrong, however. That evening, over dinner, the first real chance the three Shaws had to sit down together to talk while on French soil, Pierre du Lac was one of the very first topics of conversation her mother brought up.

"So, Nina," she said, primly arranging her napkin on her lap. "When do we get to meet this young man of yours?"

"What the heck *is* this stuff?" her father was grumbling, peering at the menu. "Pool . . . pool . . ."

"*Poulet,*" Nina said. "It's French for chicken. Don't worry, Dad. I'll order for you. I know what you like."

She only hoped the modest restaurant she had chosen for this family dinner did, indeed, serve steak, cooked medium rare, and plain baked potatoes.

"Is he in Paris?" her mother went on, not willing to be thrown off the track. "This boy, this . . . this . . . What's his name again, Nina?"

"I think you mean Pierre," Nina said. "I can understand that you're interested in meeting him," she went on, "but I don't think you understand that having met Pierre is only part of the reason I've decided to stay on in Paris. It's the city itself I can't bear to leave. I can't tell you how much I love it here. It's as if . . . as if I belong here, as if I were always meant to be here."

"Hah," her father snorted. "Now that's a silly notion, if I ever heard one. You're an American, through and through."

"I probably am," Nina replied. "But that doesn't mean I can't enjoy living in another country, or that I can't benefit from the experience of being a part of something completely different from everything I've ever known."

Her voice was gentle as she said, "You know, Dad, I probably won't end up staying here forever. You're right; I am an American. But for now, living abroad is simply what feels right to me. It's what I want."

"And college?" her father demanded. "What about that?"

"I'm not saying I won't ever go to college. I'm just not ready to go to college *yet*. At least, not back at home, in the States. I do want to take courses at the Sorbonne in the fall. I don't intend to stop learning, you know. I just want to do it my own way. And that means staying here."

"How about your friends, Kristy and Jennifer? What are their plans?"

"They're going back, just as they'd always planned." Nina couldn't resist adding, "Jennifer is like you, Mom and Dad. She can hardly stand being away from home. She's been like a fish out of water since the day she got here."

"What about money?" her father persisted. Nina could see that he had come armed with a whole list of arguments.

"I thought I'd mentioned over the telephone that I plan to get some kind of job."

"A job, huh? Doing what? A young girl like you . . . . Do you have this job yet?"

"Well, no. But I have some ideas. And I have some friends who are helping me out. Don't worry, Daddy. I'm not asking you to support me forever."

"It sounds as if you've thought of everything," Mrs. Shaw interrupted crisply. "But I still want to hear about this boy, this Pierre. Who is he? What's going on with the two of you? Surely you're not giving up college and your future and everything else that's ever meant anything to you for some teenage romance?"

It was at that point that Nina realized that all of her efforts to explain were in vain. It was a waste of time trying to make her parents understand her point of view. Her mother was absolutely right when she commented that Nina had thought of everything. Yet that fact meant nothing to either her mother or her father. All they could see was that their daughter, their little girl, was being rebellious, insisting upon doing something that they could not comprehend—and certainly not accept.

And then, all of a sudden, her mother spoke in an entirely different tone of voice. "Oh, Nina, it's just that Paris is so . . . so far away."

The intensity in her voice prompted Nina to look at her—really look at her, for the first time since her parents had arrived in Paris. And the expression on her mother's face caused her stomach to tighten.

What she saw there was fear. She realized then that what was really behind her parents' actions was not the need to control her, nor the wish to keep her a little girl. They were *afraid* for her. They were trying to protect her, trying to keep her from being hurt. And since the idea of living in another country sounded frightening to them— these two people who had never lived anywhere besides Connecticut, who rarely left Weston now that they were all settled in—they simply could not see why such an idea would hold even the slightest bit of appeal for anyone else, especially their daughter.

"Maybe we could talk about this some other time," Nina said gently, reaching over and taking her mother's hand. It hurt her to see the pained look on the woman's face, and the dampness of her mother's eyes made her insides tighten up even more. "We have plenty of time. You've only just gotten here. Let's think of tonight as a celebration—a celebration that we're all together."

Her mother just looked at her, forcing a weak smile.

After Alain learned that in the fall he would be attending college in the same city in which Kristy would be going to school, he was in such a happy mood that he went around humming all the time.

"What on earth is that noise?" Kristy asked in irritation as the two of them were taking one of their after-school strolls through the park. They were walking hand in hand. But instead of it being a romantic moment, the way it should have been, each of them seemed to be a million miles away.

"Oh, you mean my humming?" Alain asked cheerfully.

"Is that what that sound is?"

Alain shrugged. "These days, I find that I am humming all the time."

"What song is that?"

He had to think. "Oh, yes. Now I know. It is the Neil Diamond song. What do you call it? 'Coming to America.' "

When he wasn't humming, he was making plans—plans for what life would be like for him and Kristy once they were both living in the same city.

"I hope you will invite me to your parents' home for that holiday—what is it?" Alain's forehead became wrinkled as he thought hard. "The one in November, when you eat turkey and pie until you feel sick. I know. It is called Thanks-saying, right?"

"Thanksgiving," Kristy corrected him. Inwardly, she was groaning.

"Yes, that is it. Thanksgiving. It will be so exciting to have my first real American holiday—and in a huge mansion with servants, no less. Tell me, do your parents have a Rolls Royce?''

''They have six,'' she mumbled, no longer caring.

But then one day, when she met Alain at their usual time and place after her morning classes, he looked a bit troubled.

''What is it?'' she immediately asked. For the moment, at least, she forgot all about her ongoing concern about how her relationship with him was going to change—and perhaps even end—as soon as he set foot on American soil and found out that the girl he cared so much about was a total fake.

''My parents,'' he replied. ''They want to have a celebratory dinner. They want to celebrate the fact that I am going away to school in America in a few weeks. And they want to invite you. You would, in fact, be the person of honor.''

''I believe that's *guest* of honor. Why, Alain, that's very nice. I'd love to come.''

He looked at her woefully. ''I was afraid you'd say that.''

Kristy chuckled. ''That's not much of an invitation, Alain! What's the matter? Don't you want me to come to your house for dinner?''

And then suddenly she realized what his bad mood was all about. *He was embarrassed about how poor he was, compared to her!*

Of course that was the case. Here she had been carrying on all summer about how wealthy her family was, what a magnificent life-style she was used to, how she herself was practically a celebrity. And while Alain was undoubtedly impressed, he must have felt that, by comparison, his own life was modest. Perhaps he was even afraid that when she saw how simple his house and his family and his life were, she wouldn't like him anymore.

The whole situation would have been funny if Kristy hadn't been so concerned about the day that the tables were turned. She dreaded the day Alain came to visit the Connors in Weston, Connecticut. He would be expecting to see six Rolls Royces parked outside their house. Instead he would end up discovering who she really was . . . or more accurately, who she *wasn't*.

"Alain, I'd love to come to your house for dinner. And if you're worried about what I'm going to think of your family—"

"I am, a little bit," Alain said. "But that's only part of it. I am also afraid of what you will think of me once you see where I live, where I am from."

"Oh, Alain, I would never care about any of that!" she cried, and her words were more true than anything she had ever before said in her life. "Don't you understand that I like you for what you are? I don't care about how much money—or how little money—your family has. I don't care if they're not famous, or if they're not even successful. If they're good, honest, caring people, then that's all that matters."

Alain looked at her nervously. "I hope you really feel that way, Kristy. Because in a few days, on Saturday night, you will be finding out the real truth about me. My family, our store, our house, the way we all live . . . you will see all that for yourself."

Kristy reached over and took his hand. "Trust me, Alain. None of it will matter to me," she said. "Just wait. You'll see." But what she was thinking

as she gave his hand an encouraging squeeze was,
Oh, Alain, if only you end up feeling the same way
about me!

"I am so glad you decided to go out with me
this evening," Louis said warmly. "I was eager to
see you again, Jennifer, but at Claudine's party the
other night, I got the impression you weren't really certain you felt the same way about me."

Jennifer shrugged, meanwhile pulling the
sweater she was wearing more tightly around her.
She and Louis were strolling down the Boulevard
St. Germaine, headed toward a restaurant that
Louis wanted to go to. He had telephoned her a
few nights before, suggesting that the two of them
go out for coffee. She had agreed, partly because
she had felt so comfortable with him at the party,
partly because she figured it was a way to get out
of the house, to do something a little bit different.

When he arrived to pick her up, he spent a long
time with the Cartiers. Much to her surprise, he
actually seemed to enjoy talking to them. But there
was something else. He treated them with a kind
of respect, as if he were in awe of them. Jennifer
decided he was just being polite.

"Was my hunch correct?" he went on to ask.
"Were you unsure of whether or not you wanted
to see me again?"

"I guess I was feeling a little guilty, agreeing to
go out with some guy I'd met at a party when I've
got a wonderful boyfriend back home."

"Even if we are going out just as friends?"

"Well . . . that's the only reason I agreed. I
mean, it's not as if Danny were one of these pos-

sessive types who doesn't like me to have male friends."

"Tell me about him."

"Oh, Danny's great. We've been together for ages. We've even talked about getting married one day, although that's still down the road quite a bit." Dreamily, she went on. "He's really fun to be with, for one thing. He's always joking around, being the life of the party. . . . And he's really easy on the eyes, if you get what I mean."

"No, I'm afraid I don't."

"Maybe they don't say that in Kentucky. What I mean is, he's really cute. You know, good-looking."

"Ah. That, I understand."

"But that's not all. He's sweet and thoughtful. . . . I don't know, what else is there?"

Louis smiled. "It sounds as if that's enough."

"Yeah, I sure miss him. He and I have been writing to each other almost every day. He's got this really great job this summer. He's a lifeguard at the town pool." With a sigh, Jennifer added, "Boy, I sure wish I'd been with him all summer."

"Well, it is almost time for you to go back. Just another week or so, isn't it?"

"That's right," Jennifer said, showing more enthusiasm than she had all evening. "The big countdown has already begun."

"Oh, come on, Jennifer. Tell me the truth. You must be at least a little bit sad about having to leave France . . . right?"

"Me?" Jennifer laughed. "You must be kidding, Louis. I'm counting the days until I'm out of here. In fact, I'm practically counting the hours. You know, I didn't even want to come on this trip."

"No?" Louis was surprised. "Then why did you decide to come?"

"I didn't. The whole thing was my parents' idea. They thought that living abroad for the summer would make me a better person or something."

"I take it you don't agree."

"Hardly. And just as I expected, this whole summer has been nothing but a waste of time. Oh, sure, I saw a bunch of stuff, and some of it was interesting. And I guess I know more French than I did when I first got here. But all in all, I know I would have had much more fun if I'd stayed in Weston this summer."

She let out a loud sigh. "And if I wasn't crazy about the idea of coming here in the first place, I knew for sure it was a bad idea when I met the Cartiers."

"The Cartiers?" Louis's eyebrows shot up. "Why? What about them?"

"Well, it's like I was telling you at Claudine's party the other night. They're so dull. I mean, it was nice of them to invite their granddaughter Michèle up from Lyon—even though the two of us have about as much in common as a dog and a cat—but basically they're just two old people who hang around the house all day. I just don't feel they're very interesting. And wasn't that the whole idea of my coming here in the first place? So that I could meet interesting people?"

Louis opened his mouth to reply, but Jennifer cut him off before he had a chance to say a word.

"Then there are the classes we've been taking all summer. I thought they'd be a real breeze, you know? But it turns out we have to do tons of work for them. In fact, the biggest project is yet to come.

Each of us has to give an oral report the last week of class."

"I'm surprised you're going to bother."

"Huh?" Jennifer looked at him oddly. "Oh, I get it. You mean, why don't I just cut all week?"

Louis nodded.

"Don't think I haven't already considered that. But I have my two best friends to think about. Nina and Kristy. They're real gung-ho types." With a shrug, Jennifer explained, "I don't want them to think I can't do it or anything. Since they're throwing themselves into this project, I figure I ought to at least give it a try. And I don't want to make a *total* fool of myself."

"That's the spirit," Louis said.

Jennifer glanced over at him, afraid he was making fun of her. Instead, she saw that he was sincere.

"And on what topic will you be doing this oral report?"

Jennifer sighed. "That's the most boring part of all. I was assigned 'France during World War II.' "

"But that's a fascinating topic!" Louis insisted. "Very important, too."

"I guess." She didn't sound convinced. "It's just that World War II was so long ago. . . ."

Laughing, Louis protested, "It wasn't that long ago! My grandfather fought in World War II."

"It seems long ago to me. The 1940's, after all, were way before I was even born."

"But your grandparents were probably involved in it in some way, weren't they?"

"I guess." It was clear that Jennifer was already growing bored with this topic. "Look, Louis. It's nothing personal, believe me. It's just that learning about a war is not exactly my idea of a good time."

"Have you started doing any research yet?"

"A little bit. I've been doing some reading. I got a bunch of books out of the library at the Sorbonne. I'm doing my best, really. . . . It's just that the whole thing is so *dry*, you know?"

At that point, Louis stopped walking. "Well, we are here," he announced.

Jennifer's face lit up. "Oh, Louis! What a great idea! And how sweet of you to think of it!"

Louis looked around in surprise. "I'm glad you approve, Jennifer. The Café des Voix has always been one of my favorites. . . ."

"The Café de *what*?"

"The Café des Voix. Translated, it means, the café of the voices." He looked confused as he gestured toward a tiny hole in the wall, a storefront that was only as wide as a doorway and a small window. Hung over the door was a small hand-painted sign with the name of the café. "Isn't this what you were so excited about?"

Jennifer burst out laughing. "Oh, I'm sorry, Louis. I thought you were taking me over *there*!"

She pointed to a restaurant across the street. Louis's eyes followed her finger—and he saw that she was talking about the McDonald's opposite the Café des Voix.

"Oh, now I understand. I'll tell you what. I'll make a deal with you, Jennifer," he said, taking her arm and leading her toward the café. "Let's give this place, the café, a try. If you find you don't like it, then we can go to McDonald's."

"Well . . ." But already Jennifer was following him into the tiny café.

Inside it was dark and cramped, such a tiny space that it was almost like being in someone's living room. The wall that ran the length of the long, narrow room was exposed brick. Hung on it were the front pages of newspapers, displayed in picture frames. Jennifer's French was good enough for her to figure out that their headlines were calls to action. Many of them were from the late 1960's, a time she knew had been one of great political activism in France, especially with the students. But most of them, she saw, were very recent.

The café was packed. There were only a dozen or so tables, rough wooden tables without any tablecloths. Six or eight young people, not much older than she was, were huddled around each table, drinking small cups of coffee that looked like espresso. Most of them were talking loudly or even arguing. All of them seemed very intense.

"This looks like a place that girl Monique would love," Jennifer said to Louis. There were no rugs to absorb any of the sound, nothing but bare wooden floors, and so she was forced to talk loudly in order to be heard.

Louis laughed. "As a matter of fact, this is where I first met her. She comes here at least twice a week."

"What exactly goes on here?"

"It's called the Café des Voix because it's a place for people to come and discuss the various issues they care about. It started in the sixties, when students at the Sorbonne created a sort of rebellion here in the city. But its tradition has lived on. This café has become a hangout for people who are active politically, people who are involved in issues like ecology, improving human rights, solving the problem of world hunger, freeing political prisoners. . . ."

He looked at Jennifer questioningly. "Well, what do you think? There seems to be one table that's free, over there in the corner. Shall we grab it?"

But she made a face. "If you don't mind, Louis, I'd rather go somewhere else. I'm afraid this just isn't my kind of place."

As he walked her across the street, toward McDonald's, Louis took her arm once again. This time, however, he was muttering, talking more to himself than to Jennifer. "Ah, Jennifer," he was saying with a chuckle, "perhaps you are a hopeless case, after all." Then, more seriously—and much more meaningfully—he added, "But perhaps not. That, I suspect, still remains to be seen."

11

"WHERE ON EARTH ARE WE *GOING*?" JEN-
nifer demanded, not even trying to mask her exasperation.

"We already told you," Michèle replied calmly.
"Louis and I want it to be a surprise."

"Great, just great," Jennifer mumbled. She
folded her arms across her chest and frowned.
"Why is it I get the distinct feeling that this 'surprise' is probably not one I'm going to be thrilled
about?"

It was a few days after her date with Louis, the
one that had begun at the Café des Voix and ended
at one of Paris's branches of McDonald's, where
she happily downed two cheeseburgers, a chocolate shake, and a large order of French fries. Louis
had watched in amazement, sipping coffee from a
paper cup.

Jennifer had gotten the feeling that he was
studying her, that the questions he kept asking her
were more than simply a way of being friendly.
She felt as if she were a specimen in biology class,
placed under the microscope for the class to ex-
amine.

And now this. Early on this Saturday morning,
Michèle had come into her room to wake her up,
saying in her usual cheerful voice that she and

Louis had planned an outing, a way of marking her last weekend in Paris. Sure enough; as they emerged from the Cartiers' apartment building, onto the street, Louis was waiting for them at the curb in a car he had borrowed for the day.

Yet the two of them remained secretive. On the surface, it looked as if everything were fine. There was a large basket on the back seat, beside Jennifer, and when she peeked inside she saw a perfectly innocent-looking picnic lunch. Michèle and Louis, meanwhile, sitting in the front seat, were armed with maps and guide books steering them to the Loire Valley, south of Paris.

What could be more fun than a day in the country, especially a sunny, warm summer day like this one? Jennifer asked herself. Even so, she couldn't shake the feeling that something was up.

"The Loire Valley," she commented once the car had left the crowded streets of the city, winding its way south on a highway with traffic that was much lighter than the usual congestion of Paris. "Isn't that the area of France where all the castles are?"

"That's right." Louis, glancing at her through the rearview mirror, looked pleased that, somewhere along the way, she had absorbed at least one tidbit of information about the country she was living in. "There are many magnificent *châteaux* along the Loire River. Touring some of them is a wonderful experience."

"I just hope that's the 'wonderful experience' these two have cooked up for me," Jennifer muttered.

She lapsed into silence as Louis and Michèle chatted together in the front seat. Sometimes they spoke in English and sometimes in French; sometimes they attempted to include her in their conversation, and other times they acted as if she weren't even there.

What do I care? Jennifer thought, staring out the window, noting how the scenery changed as they drove farther from the city, deeper into the countryside. I'll be leaving in a few days, anyway. I'll never have to see Michèle or Louis or the Cartiers again. So why should I start worrying about what they think of me *now*?

Despite her refusal to think of this little outing as anything that came even close to fun, Jennifer had to admit that it was pretty out here. The crowdedness of the city and the area surrounding it was replaced by large fields and quaint farmhouses. Every once in a while they drove through a small town, two or three dozen tiny buildings pushed together along a cobblestone street. In a way, it was like going back in time. Everything felt old . . . and untouched, as if someone had decided to preserve something of value, a little piece of an age gone by.

"This sure is a long ride," Jennifer commented when the threesome had been riding in the car for almost an hour. She was getting bored with driving through the country, no matter how pretty it was. She was also getting a little tired of feeling as if she were being kidnapped. "I guess we'll be getting close to some of those castles soon."

"Oh, we're not going to look at any castles," Louis replied, glancing at her over his shoulder. "But we will be at our destination soon."

Jennifer opened her mouth to ask, once again, where they were going. But she quickly snapped it shut, realizing that there was really no point in asking the question that her two captors were so determined not to answer.

She found out soon enough. Louis pulled the car off the main road, onto a small dirt road that was actually little more than a path. She perked up, sitting up straighter and looking out the window. She expected to see something wonderful, a museum or a park or—despite what Louis had said—a castle. Instead, all that was out there was a ramshackle old farmhouse.

"What's this, my big chance to see how the farmers of France live?" Jennifer asked dryly.

She took in the overgrown fields surrounding the house, making it look as if no one had lived there or cared about the place for years. The house itself was in pretty tumbledown condition as well. It reminded her of a haunted house in some low-budget movie. One of the windows on the second floor was broken. The front door looked as if one good gust of wind could knock it off its hinges. Despite herself, Jennifer shuddered.

"Okay, you guys. What's this all about?" she asked. "Am I supposed to be scared or something?"

Michèle glanced back at her in surprise as Louis pulled the car up right in front and turned off the motor.

"This is the house where my grandparents used to live," she said matter-of-factly.

"Oh, is *that* all." Jennifer was disappointed.

It figures that these two would think it was a big deal to drive forever and a day just so they could go see some old shack that the Cartiers used to live in, she was thinking. As if anybody would ever give two hoots. *Especially* me.

But Louis and Michèle were already climbing out of the car.

"Come inside," Louis said in a friendly way. "There is something interesting I would like to show you."

Reluctantly Jennifer followed them into the house. I just hope there aren't any mice in there, she was thinking. Or anything *worse* than mice . . . .

She was relieved to find that, inside, the house was clean and almost pleasant. The sun was shining through the windows, and a few pieces of furniture that had been left behind made it look almost homey.

"Okay. So we've seen it," she announced, after taking a quick tour of the first floor. "There's a living room, a kitchen, and a bedroom. Very nice. Can we go home now?"

"You have not seen the entire house yet," Michèle said in a strange voice.

"What else is there to see?" Jennifer returned. "Some dusty old attic full of spiders? A damp old basement?"

Michèle smiled oddly. "Something like that."

She went over to the spot where a large, heavy, and not very nice-looking cabinet was sitting. Louis joined her in her efforts to make it budge, the two of them throwing all their weight against it. Finally they managed to move it across the room a few feet. Underneath there was a small square cut out of the floor.

"A trapdoor?" Jennifer asked with interest. "What's it for?"

Instead of answering her, Louis and Michèle

pulled the heavy door open. Then they gestured for her to look inside.

Jennifer was a little nervous as she walked over, not sure of what she would see. And what she did see as she peered over the edge of the opening was so unexpected that she didn't know how to react.

"Why, there are rooms down there! It's kind of like a little apartment!" she exclaimed. "It's almost as if there's another whole house underneath this one. A secret house. But, gosh, who on earth would ever want to live under the ground?"

She looked at them, puzzled.

"Louis, Michèle, what is all this about?" she asked. This time, however, there was none of the usual defiance in her voice. "What does this mean?"

"This is the house in which my grandparents were living during World War II," Michèle said in a quiet voice. "My grandfather built this hiding place all by himself."

"A hiding place? What for?"

This time, it was Louis who answered her question. "During the war, the Cartiers hid members of the French Resistance here in their home. This house was a safe place for people who were secretly working against the Nazis, who, of course, had taken over France, occupying the country, claiming it as their own. For almost two years there was activity here aimed at ridding France of the Nazis. This was, in fact, one of the major outposts of the Resistance movement."

"The Cartiers hid people here?" Jennifer repeated, not quite understanding what she was hearing. "But . . . but wasn't that dangerous?"

"It was extremely dangerous," Michèle replied.

"If they had ever been caught by the Nazis, they surely would have been put to death. My grandparents put themselves at incredible risk every minute, every second of the day, for almost two years."

"But why did they do it?" Jennifer asked in amazement.

"Because they believed in something," Louis said. "Because they knew they were right. And because they knew that they could make a difference."

Jennifer was quiet for a long time. Suddenly, she understood everything. Why Louis and Michèle had brought her here, why they had always been so respectful of the Cartiers, why they were so resentful of Jennifer's inability to see them as anything more than a pair of old people, people she kept referring to as "boring." And she also understood the commitment these two young people, people her own age, had made to becoming involved in some of the things that really mattered.

Like the Cartiers, people like Louis and Michèle and Monique and the people at the Café des Voix knew they could make a difference.

As the three of them took a brief tour of the grounds surrounding the house, with Michèle and Louis pointing out different places that had been a part of the Cartiers' fight against the Nazis during World War II, Jennifer remained silent, thinking hard. She was embarrassed by the way she had been behaving all along, ever since she had come to France. Even more than that, she was awed by what she had learned.

Finally, she turned to her friends and said, "I

think I've seen enough now. Do you think we could go back to Paris?"

Her voice sounded much less certain as she added, "Now that I've seen . . . all this, now that I understand, I'm eager to talk to the Cartiers. I have a feeling there's a lot I could learn from them."

Louis and Michèle just looked at each other and smiled.

"I-I guess I owe the two of you an apology," Jennifer stammered in her awkward French.

"An apology?" Madame Cartier looked surprised. She and her husband were sitting at the kitchen table, sharing an apple that had been carefully cut into slices.

Her husband was just as confused. "Why, Jennifer? What have you done?"

Jennifer glanced over at Michèle and Louis, standing right behind her. Michèle gave her an encouraging nod. "What I've done," she said slowly, "is forget that there are other people in the world. Besides me, I mean."

Henri Cartier frowned. *"Pardon?"* he said. "Please explain."

"Ever since I got here, all I've thought about has been myself." Jennifer was quiet for a few seconds. "Come to think of it, that's pretty much what I've always done.

"Madame Cartier, Monsieur Cartier, I want you both to know that I appreciate all the effort you've gone to. Inviting Michèle, someone my own age, to Paris . . . trying to make me feel at home. . . . You've been so thoughtful. And I've been acting like a . . . like a spoiled little girl."

"Jennifer," Madame Cartier said, coming over and grasping both her hands, "you have not done anything to offend us. We understand that it is difficult for someone to travel so far away from home, so far away from everything that is familiar."

"Yes, I know you understand. As a matter of fact, I know a lot of things now." Jennifer took a deep breath. "Madame, Monsieur, today Michèle and Louis took me out to the Loire Valley. To the farmhouse where you used to live."

The muscles of the older woman's hands tightened.

"They told me everything. All about what happened during World War II, the risks you took, the brave things you did."

Madame Cartier glanced at her husband. The two of them exchanged a look of sadness.

"More than anything," Jennifer went on, "I owe both of you an apology because up until now I never even tried to look far enough beyond myself to see you for who you really are."

"And now?" Madame Cartier said in a soft voice.

"And now," Jennifer said, giving the older woman's hands a squeeze, "I am ready to listen."

"Tonight's the night," Kristy muttered, gulping loudly as she closed the front door of her host family's house behind her. "This dinner at Alain's parents' house could be a beautiful beginning for us. Or else . . . or else it could be the end."

For days she had been dreading this evening. In fact, it had been pretty much all she could think about ever since Alain had first told her about his family's plan to hold a celebratory dinner. His mother and father were quite eager to meet his new American friend, he reported happily, especially now that he was going to be off to the States himself in just a few short weeks.

She could imagine how excited Alain's parents were for their son, even despite their initial reservations. And she could imagine how much this family dinner meant to them, too. Such sweet, simple folk, about to see their son take off on his own and follow a new path . . . Why, they had probably even closed up their little shop, just for the occasion.

Kristy had dressed carefully, choosing a simple, attractive dress. And she hadn't wanted to show up empty handed. She had given a lot of thought to what to bring. She didn't want to bring anything so expensive it would embarrass them, yet she was still playing the part of the wealthy film star, and she didn't want to give away her true status before she had a chance to tell Alain the truth herself. In the end, she had gone into a department store called Le Grand Magasin, Paris's third largest and easily the fanciest, and bought a very expensive box of their most exclusive chocolates.

In fact, it was that box of Le Grand Magasin candy that Alain first noticed when she met him near the métro station so that he could accompany her to his parents' house on the outskirts of the city.

"What is this?" he asked, amused.

"What do you think it is?" Kristy returned. "It's a box of chocolates for your parents. You know, a little thank-you gift." Her expression darkened. "Why, don't you think they'll like it? I mean, do you think it's too . . . too showy?"

"Showy?" Alain repeated, his face reflecting his bewilderment.

"You know, showy. Um, too expensive, trying too hard to impress somebody. . . ."

Alain laughed. "No, Kristy, I think they will like this present very much. It was a charming idea."

Feeling relieved, she tucked the box of candy under her arm and started down the steps into the métro station with Alain at her side.

"You know, Alain, I'm kind of nervous about tonight," she admitted.

"Oh, do not worry. My parents will like you very much."

"I'm sure I'll like them, too. But that's not what I'm worried about."

Just then, Alain turned to face her. He was wearing a distracted expression, as if he hadn't really been paying very close attention to what she had been saying.

"Tell me, Kristy. How do you feel about surprises?"

Kristy, caught completely off guard, glanced over at Alain.

"That's funny, Alain. I was just going to ask you the same thing."

"Really? Why is that?"

"I . . . uh, oh, never mind." There would be plenty of time for that later. *More* than enough, she thought woefully.

Kristy was grateful that a subway train was just pulling into the métro station, and the two of them rushed to get on it. She was, meanwhile, so wrapped up in her own nervousness about the evening ahead—and the reaction that her confession was bound to cause—that she forgot all about

Alain's question about how she felt about surprises almost as soon as he mentioned it.

But his words came back to her a few minutes later as the two of them got off the métro in the neighborhood called Neuilly. This was a section of Paris she hadn't visited before. It was residential, but it contained within its tree-lined streets some of the finest homes she had seen so far in Paris. The high-priced boutiques the two of them passed as they made their way deeper and deeper into this neighborhood supported Kristy's realization that Alain's house—and his family—were not going to be quite what she had been expecting.

"Is your parents' house around here?" she asked, trying to sound casual.

"Yes, it is not too far."

"I see." After hesitating for a few moments, Kristy added, "I guess I was expecting a more modest neighborhood."

Alain glanced over at her nervously. "I hope this does not bother you?"

"Oh, no, no, not at all," she was quick to assure him. "It's just . . . a bit of a surprise."

But her initial reaction to the neighborhood in which Alain and his family lived was nothing compared to her astonishment when Alain finally stopped walking and announced, "Well, Kristy, this is it. This is my house."

For a few seconds, she thought he was joking. But the serious expression on his face told her right away that that was not the case. The house before her was more of a mansion than anything else. It was a large, gray, three-story brick town house, much larger than any of the others she had seen, even in this elegant neighborhood. There was a circular driveway in front, and in it there were parked two of the most expensive sports cars Kristy had ever seen. Everywhere there were manicured shrubs and flowering plants in large pots, and an ornate black wrought-iron fence outlined what looked like quite a large plot of land.

"Whoa!" Kristy breathed.

"You don't like it?" Alain asked anxiously.

"No, it's wonderful. It's just . . . bigger than what I thought."

"Come inside. I'm sure my parents are waiting for us."

Sure enough; Alain's parents were sitting in the living room. The two of them made a well-dressed, dignified couple, who looked very much at home in their lush surroundings. Alain's father wore a well-cut suit; his mother, meanwhile, was a beautiful woman in a beige silk dress. Their elegant clothing perfectly complemented the fine furnishings of their home: thick oriental carpets, antique furniture, huge oil paintings, a grand piano.

"You must be Kristy!" Alain's mother cried, coming toward the young couple as they walked in the front door. Kristy only hoped she could remember to keep from staring as she took all this in. She was relieved that she did, at least, have the presence of mind to look Alain's mother in the eye and smile.

And then she found herself doing a double take. This woman was the actress that had starred in the movie she and Alain had seen together!

"We are so pleased to meet you," Charlotte LePage, the most popular movie actress in all of France, went on. "Alain has talked about you so much. And now that he is going to Massachusetts in the fall to study rocks. . . ."

"Geology, *maman*," Alain corrected her gently.

"Whatever." Charlotte waved her arms in the air. "Anyway, it is so nice that he will already have a friend who is living near him."

Suddenly she noticed the box that Kristy was clutching. "What is this?" she asked, puzzled.

"Oh. I almost forgot. I brought you these." Kristy handed the box of Le Grand Magasin chocolates to her hostess. But instead of looking pleased, the expression on Charlotte LePage's face was one of confusion.

As if to explain, Alain said, "*Maman*, Kristy brought these as a little present for you. She thought it would be a nice gesture."

Still looking puzzled, Alain's mother accepted the box of candy. "Thank you, Kristy," she said, putting it aside on a small table. "*Merci.*"

"Well, Alain, Kristy," Alain's father said, "I believe dinner will be served shortly. I hope you like duck à l'orange, truffles, and crème caramel."

Kristy just nodded. By this point she was so overwhelmed that she couldn't have gotten out any words even if she had wanted to.

"Yes, dinner should be ready," Charlotte said. "Lucille and Anna have been working all day. In fact, I think I will go and check on things, if you will pardon me." She hurried out of the room, obviously anxious that her dinner party go well.

"And if you will excuse me for a moment," Alain's father said, "I must make a telephone call." He sighed. "There was a problem with a shipment of diamonds," he explained. "Some sort of delay. . . . My customers will not like this at all!''

Once they were alone, Kristy sneaked a peek over at Alain. He was standing on the other side of the room, watching her, clearly anxious to see what her reaction to all this was going to be.

''Alain,'' she said evenly, ''just out of curiosity, what's the name of your parents' store? The one your father owns?''

Alain paled. ''Uh, Le Grand Magasin.''

''Le Grand Magasin.'' Kristy swallowed hard. ''I see. That's the little neighborhood shop your family runs.''

''We only have six branches,'' he offered apologetically.

''And your mother? She is the actress who was in that movie we saw, the one you did everything in your power to keep me from seeing, right?''

He nodded guiltily. ''Perhaps you understand now why I asked you earlier if you liked surprises.''

Suddenly Kristy burst out into loud, uncontrollable laughter. But the tears in her eyes weren't from laughing so hard.

''Kristy! Are you all right? I can't tell if you're laughing or crying!''

''Neither can I,'' she gasped. ''Actually, I'm probably doing a little bit of both.''

''Then you are very angry with me.'' Alain was frowning. ''You are very—what is the word?—disappointed.''

''No, Alain. I'm not disappointed. And I'm not angry, either.''

''You're not? Oh, Kristy. I am so relieved.'' He still looked puzzled. ''But you are not even a *little* bit angry? After all, I was not completely honest with you."

"No, I guess you weren't, were you?" Kristy was pretending she was annoyed, but there was a definite twinkle in her eyes.

"I am so sorry. It is just that . . . well, to be honest, I was afraid that if you knew the truth about who I was—who my family was—you wouldn't like me for myself. So many times, there had been girls who pretended to like me, when really what they liked was the fact that my parents were well known, or that we had money, or that. . . ."

"Or that you were someone so important that you have journalists coming up to you at sidewalk cafés, begging you for an exclusive interview?"

Alain's mouth dropped open. "That was the very first time you and I had lunch together. You mean you knew that that man was a journalist? You knew he was from a magazine, and that he was looking for a story?"

"I didn't know it at the time." Kristy was chuckling. "But now it all snaps into place."

"It snaps . . . into *what*?"

"I understand now. What was going on at the time, I mean."

Alain just nodded. "I am so very happy that you are not mad at me, Kristy. I know that all along, I have been lying to you. But I meant no harm. I just wanted to try being someone else for a change. To try being someone from a normal family, just once. I wanted to see how that felt . . . and I wanted to see if someone could like me for who I am. Someone nice, someone . . . someone like you.

"And I am also happy that all of this—" he gestured with both hands at the grand surroundings that he called home"—does not make you feel uncomfortable."

Suddenly he remembered something. "But, wait a moment! Here I am forgetting who you are. Of course you are not impressed by all this. You, after all, come from a very similar background—"

"Uh, Alain," Kristy interrupted. "I think you'd better sit down. There's something I have to explain."

With a nod of his head, Alain sat down on the edge of an elegant, hand-carved wooden chair upholstered with gold brocade fabric. He was looking at her expectantly, curious about what she had to tell him, now that it was her turn.

"Once upon a time, there was a very ordinary girl who led what she considered a very ordinary life," she began. "At least that was what she thought until she found out there were some things, like taking pictures, that she could do very well. . . ."

Oddly enough, Kristy discovered that she didn't feel nervous at all as she started telling Alain her "secret"—the one she had been keeping from him all summer. In fact, she couldn't remember the last time she had felt so good.

The first few days of the Shaws' visit were even more difficult than Nina had expected. Her parents played the role of tourist with great reluctance. They resisted her attempts at showing them Paris, at helping them have fun, at making them appreciate the city she loved so much.

Even as she led them around the famous sights, they were unwilling to act as if they were having a good time. The Eiffel Tower, they reported, was smaller than they had expected it to be. Notre-Dame was too crowded; the Seine was polluted; and everything in the entire city was much too expensive.

All the while her parents kept asking about Pierre, hinting that they wanted to meet him. But Nina wasn't ready for that. Instead, she made excuses, insisting that he was tied up or out of town.

She did, however, arrange for them to have dinner with Jennifer and Kristy. Nina knew her parents would feel comfortable with them. After all, the girls were so familiar to her mother and father that they were like a breath of fresh air, a little bit of home here on distant shores.

Even their little dinner party, however, wasn't completely free of tension.

"I know exactly how you feel, Mr. and Mrs. Shaw," Jennifer said heartily, helping herself to another breadstick as the five of them sat crowded together at a tiny Italian restaurant. Just that afternoon, Nina's mother had announced that if she was forced to eat another morsel of French food, something she was guaranteed not to be able to identify, she was going to scream. "When I first got to France, I wasn't exactly thrilled, either. And the truth of the matter is, I can't wait to get back home. But even I got to the point where I realized there's something to gain from every experience, even one that makes you feel a little uncomfortable at first."

"I'm sure Nina never felt uncomfortable here in the least," Kristy said, trying to be helpful. "She had no problem getting used to being on French soil at all. And by the time she's been living here for a few months—"

"Uh, that still hasn't been completely decided,"
Mr. Shaw interrupted. "The three of us are still
talking about it."

Kristy took a deep breath. "Well, I think you
may change your minds when you hear the little
tidbit of news I've got." Turning to Nina, Kristy
went on, "Remember how you had everything all
set—except a job?"

"Yes. . . ." Nina could feel her heart beginning
to pound as she waited to hear what Kristy had to
say.

"Well, Nina, I got you a job!"

"You *what*?"

"That's right. That is, if you want it. How would
you like to be the personal assistant to France's
most famous—and best-loved—movie actress?
Charlotte LePage, her name is. And she was com-
plaining to me over dinner just the other night that
she's so busy trying to juggle her schedule, star-
ring in movies and writing a book about her life
and doing lots of public appearances for charities,
that she just has to find somebody reliable, smart,
organized. . . . " Kristy shrugged. "I told her all
about you, Nina, and she's dying to meet you."

After that night, Nina's parents were even more
tight lipped. She could tell they were feeling as if
they were being backed into a corner, as if too
much was happening too fast—for them as well as
for their daughter. But Nina continued to stick to
her guns. While at one time she had been afraid
that her parents might be able to talk her out of
her plan to stay on in Paris, seeing that their caution was based more on fear of the unknown than
anything real made her more determined than

ever. While the three of them weren't discussing their conflict every minute they were together—in fact, they were barely talking about it at all—it was no secret to any of them that whether Nina would stay on was first and foremost on everyone's mind.

Finally, on their fifth day in Paris, after Nina had already taken them to every museum, cathedral, and monument she could find in the guidebooks, she could stand the tension no more.

"Look, Mom and Dad," she said as they sat together on a bench in the Bois de Boulogne, resting.

It was, in fact, the same bench that she and Pierre always used as their meeting place—"their bench," as they thought of it. She had brought her parents here to the Bois only as a last resort, preferring to keep this place special in her own mind but having run out of other choices of how to keep them busy for an entire afternoon.

"It's really been fun, showing you two around," she went on. "But I know that the whole time, you've been agonizing over my decision to stay on in Paris after the summer is over."

"Are you still thinking about that?" her father returned. "Since you hadn't said anything, I figured you'd forgotten all about that ridiculous idea."

"No, Dad, I haven't." Nina's voice was low and controlled. "And I don't think it's a ridiculous idea at all."

"Nina, you simply cannot do this," her father returned, his anger escalating. "It's . . . it's crazy. I want you to stop talking about this right now. You've always been a sensible girl, and I'm not going to let you start getting silly now, not when college and your future and everything else are all set."

Nina, feeling her eyes well up with tears, turned to her mother. "Oh, Mom!" she cried. "Can't you help me? Can't you help me make Daddy understand?"

"No, Nina, I can't," her mother returned coldly. "Because I happen to agree with him one hundred percent."

"Look, I've had about enough of this," Mr. Shaw said, standing up. "I . . . I need a walk. I'm going back to the hotel."

With that, he stormed off, heading toward the exit of the park.

Nina and her mother remained silent for a long time, sitting together on the bench. And then, suddenly, Nina knew what she had to do.

"Mom," she said, "I know you don't agree with me on this, and I know you don't understand. But will you please do me one favor?"

"What's that?" Mrs. Shaw asked uneasily.

"Come back to the Rousseaus' house with me." She took a deep breath. "There's . . . there's something there that I want to show you.

Nina's heart was pounding like a jackhammer by then. Part of her felt reckless, as if she were about to betray a confidence that she had been trusted with. But at the same time, another part of her knew that, given the circumstances, her grandmother would never have disapproved of what she was about to do.

Mrs. Shaw sat perched on the edge of her daughter's bed at the Rousseaus' house. Her body was tense as she read the letters that, once upon a time, a young man named Marcel du Lac had written to a beautiful young American woman named Anna Wentworth.

Nina, meanwhile, leaned against the window-sill, her eyes glued to her mother's face. And she saw there what she had been hoping to see: that her mother's expression changed from one of skepticism and confusion to one of understanding and sympathy.

The two of them were silent for a long time, sitting together in the same room, the mother reading, the daughter waiting. When Mrs. Shaw finally looked up after having read the last letter in the pile, her eyes were wet. Slowly she folded the letter up and placed it back in its envelope. She was treating the piece of paper with a kind of reverence, as if it were something fragile, something worthy of respect.

Her expression was sheepish as she glanced at her daughter. "I never knew about any of this," she said in a voice that was hoarse with emotion. "It explains so much. That sadness that always seemed to be with her, no matter what else she was doing. The way her eyes would light up on those few occasions when she talked about the time she had spent in Paris. The way she would sit in the garden, surrounded by all those yellow roses, with that dreamy, faraway look in her eyes. . . ."

Her voice trailed off. Never before had Nina heard that tone in her mother's voice, and she had never seen such a soft, romantic look on her face. It was as if she had uncovered a whole different side of her, one that Nina had never before been allowed to see. She wondered if perhaps her mother herself had even forgotten that that side of her existed.

"Thank you for letting me see these," Mrs. Shaw went on. "I can see that they mean a lot to you."

Nina sat down on the opposite edge of the bed. "I am hoping that they will help you understand what staying on in Paris means to me."

Gently she took the letters from her mother and placed them on the bed, between the two of them. "My grandmother—your mother—wasn't able to stay in Paris, to see if her love with Marcel was real, to explore what her life could have been like if she had felt free to follow her dreams. She was too tied to convention, too afraid to break free of her family's expectations of her. But things are different now—"

"Some things haven't changed," her mother interrupted.

Nina looked at her, confused.

"What hasn't changed is that mothers still want the best for their daughters. They want to protect them, to keep them safe. . . ." She reached over and took Nina's hand. "And maybe to hold on to them just a little bit longer than they should."

Mrs. Shaw's face softened into a smile. "You're right, Nina. You do have to do what you feel in your heart. What your father and I want for you can't always be the same as what you want for yourself. You're a young woman now, not a child. And it is time for you to start making decisions for yourself."

"Then you agree that it's okay if I stay?" Nina gasped, not quite able to believe she was hearing her mother correctly.

Mrs. Shaw nodded. "Yes, Nina. I can see now

that I was wrong. I'll do whatever I can to help you."

"I know one thing you can do," Nina said with a frown. "You can talk to Daddy. Try to make him understand."

"Yes, I'll even do that." Mrs. Shaw laughed. "I don't think your father is the romantic type, but I do know one thing. Every time you and I stand firm in our beliefs, we manage to win him over." She chuckled again, then added, "Well, sooner or later, anyway."

"Oh, Mom, thank you." Nina leaned over and gave her mother a big hug. "I wanted you to understand. I wanted you to know how important this was to me."

"I do now," her mother replied.

When the two of them pulled apart, Mrs. Shaw was smiling. "Now, Nina, does this mean I finally get to meet this young man of yours? The one you've been hiding from us?"

Nina laughed. "Yes, Mom. I'd love it if you and Dad met Pierre."

"I'm sure he must be very special" Mrs. Shaw said. Thoughtfully, she added, "Just like his grandfather."

12

"*THERE* YOU ARE, YOU TWO! THANK GOODness! I was afraid I'd missed the plane!"

Jennifer came running across Charles de Gaulle Airport, dragging along her two heavy suitcases. She was headed toward Gate 12, the departure point for Air France Flight 77, Paris to New York City, scheduled to leave in less than an hour.

Nina and Kristy, lingering in front of the dutyfree gift shop, looked at each other and laughed.

"I guess some things never change, do they?" Kristy said, still chuckling.

Suddenly she grew serious. "But there is one thing that has changed. Jennifer and I may be going back home in an hour, but you won't be coming with us."

Nina's smile faded. It was as if, all of a sudden, the magnitude of what she was doing hit her. Two fat tears drifted down her cheeks.

"Oh, Kristy, I'm so scared!" she cried, her voice barely a whisper.

"I know you are." Kristy leaned over and threw her arms around her friend. "Anybody in your shoes would be scared to death."

"Really?" As she hugged her back, burying her face in her shoulder, Nina sounded as if she didn't quite believe her.

"Sure. You're about to begin the biggest adventure of your life. A new city, a new job, a new apartment, a new boyfriend . . ."

"There's one *old* thing I'm going to miss very, very much."

"What's that?"

As Nina drew away, her expression was one of surprise. "Why, my old friends, of course!"

Neither of them spoke for the next few seconds. But the looks on both their faces said much more than mere words ever could.

"Are you guys still here?"

Jennifer was back, still clutching her suitcases— and looking very impatient.

"We were supposed to meet Ms. Darcy and the others at the gate about fifteen minutes ago," she said. "She's going to have a cow if we don't show up there soon."

"Give me a break, Jen," Kristy replied. "I'm not going to see Nina again for a long time."

"Oh, Nina will be back, at least to visit, in no time. Right?" Jennifer added anxiously.

Nina couldn't help laughing. "I guess I'll have to come back, if I'm going to get to see *you*. I know I'd better not hold my breath until you hop on a plane and come over to Europe again!"

"Oh, it's not so bad here, once you get used to it," Jennifer said loftily. "It's even possible for a person to learn a thing or two—if she's open to it, that is."

"Well, Jen," Kristy interjected, an impish look on her face, "there's plenty of room in Nina's apartment. With a little bit of reshuffling, I bet that one more person could fit in there without any problem. So it's not too late for you to change your mind about getting on that plane and going back home—"

"Are you kidding?" Jennifer squealed. "I can't wait!" Dreamily, she added, "Danny's promised to be waiting for me at the airport with a dozen red roses."

"Like I said before," Kristy commented, grinning, "I guess some things never change."

"There are some things I hope *never* change."

All three girls turned at the unexpected sound of the male voice that had suddenly broken into their conversation. They saw that they had been joined by two of their favorite Parisians.

"Pierre!" Nina cried with delight. "You made it!"

"Of course! I wanted to be with you while you said good-bye to your two American friends." Pierre slipped his hand in hers. "I thought you could probably use a Parisian friend right about now."

Nina gave his hand a grateful squeeze. She was pleased that he understood.

"I just hope Nina doesn't regret her decision," said Alain, who had come over to Kristy and put his arm around her. "I can practically guarantee that working for my mother isn't going to be any barbecue."

"Barbecue?" The three girls looked at each other, puzzled. And then Kristy burst out laughing.

"I think you mean it won't be any *picnic*!"

Alain just looked bewildered. "Ah, your language is so difficult."

"Don't worry, Alain," Nina said reassuringly. "You'll have plenty of time to learn it. In just a couple of weeks, you'll be living in Boston."

"I know. Not far from my favorite English teacher." He was gazing fondly at Kristy. In a teasing voice, he added, "You know, the one who doesn't own a single Rolls Royce but has still managed to drive away with my heart."

"Well, I hate to be a wet blanket," Jennifer cut in, "or as Alain would say, a damp comforter. . . ."

"Or a moist afghan," Kristy teased.

"Or a mildewed sleeping bag," Nina added.

"Anyway, you guys, we'd better get a move on. I'm dying to get on that plane."

"I guess it is almost time." Kristy turned to face Alain. "Well, I guess I'll be seeing you soon."

Alain nodded. "We don't even have to say good-bye."

"We don't, either," Pierre whispered in Nina's ear. Once again, she gave his hand a squeeze.

"So it looks like this is it." Jennifer gave Nina a long look, then threw her arms around her. "Have a great time, kid!"

Next she faced Pierre. "And you make sure she's okay, all right?"

"You've got my promise."

"Okay, enough. Let's get going before I burst into tears," Kristy said. She blinked hard, took a few deep breaths, and then tossed her head. "Come on, Jen. Like you've been saying, we don't want that plane to take off without us."

She picked up her own suitcase, turned away, and then peeked over her shoulder at Nina.

"Catch you later," she said lightly. And then she was off.

"Are you okay?" Jennifer asked in a soft voice, glancing over at Kristy as the two of them hurried toward the gate.

"I'm great," Kristy replied. "Really. I'm happy for Nina. She got what she wanted."

"You should be happy for yourself, too," Jennifer pointed out. "Don't forget, you also got what you wanted."

Slowly a smile crept across Kristy's face. "Yes, I guess you're right," she said. "I did get what I wanted."

Nina, meanwhile, stayed behind with Pierre and Alain, watching her two best friends as they walked away. Instead of feeling sad or being on the verge of tears, the way she would have expected, she found she was actually smiling. She was experiencing a sense of warmth and security from just knowing she had such good friends—no matter how far away they might be.

"Do you want to stay?" Pierre asked gently. "We could watch the plane take off."

"No, that's all right." Nina gave her friends one last look, then turned to him. "I'm ready to go."

They began walking out of the airport, with Pierre at Nina's side and Alain a few paces behind.

"Do you feel as if something in your life has just come to an end?" Pierre asked in a soft voice.

"In a way," Nina replied.

She thought for a few moments before adding, "But do you know what? What I feel even more strongly is that something else is about to begin."

About the Author

Cynthia Blair grew up on Long Island, New York, and attended Bryn Mawr College in Pennsylvania, where she earned her bachelor's degree. She earned her master's degree from M.I.T. and worked as a manager for food companies before abandoning the corporate life in order to write. She lives on Long Island with her husband and son.

Carla Farrell seems like a happy-go-lucky kid, but her insecurities make her a compulsive eater. Because she is too fat to be a romantic lead, she loses a part in the school play that her acting talent deserves. Carla is more jealous than ever of her thin, glamorous, perfect sister Kelly, who gets a job at the coolest store in the mall. Then a bracelet disappears, and Kelly is accused of stealing it. With the help of the Bubble Gum Gang, Carla investigates the theft and finds out that even perfect people have problems in

CHOCOLATE IS MY MIDDLE NAME

by Cynthia Blair

Coming in September 1992 from Fawcett Books.

CYNTHIA BLAIR

Available in bookstores everywhere from Fawcett Books.